He Went With

Drake

Publisher's Note

He Went With Drake was written over 60 years ago and tells the story of a young man accompanying Drake on his adventures around the world.

An excellent storyteller, Louise Andrews Kent provides the reader with the opportunity to experience a different time and place through the eyes of the main character, including the social customs, religious beliefs, and racial relations. Taking place over 400 years ago, many parts of life are foreign and sometimes offensive to us now, including specific customs, practices, beliefs, and words. To maintain and provide historical accuracy and to allow a true representation of this time period the words used and the customs and attitudes described have not been removed or edited.

This edition published 2022
by Living Book Press

ISBN: 978-1-922634-95-5 (hardcover)
        978-1-922634-94-8 (softcover)

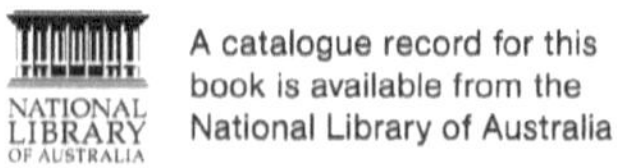

He Went With

Drake

LOUISE ANDREWS KENT

ILLUSTRATED BY
ROBERT BEARS MACLEAN

Living Book Press

CONTENTS

CHAPTER 1

CAMPIONS'

WHEN OLIVER Barrett opened the door of his father's work-shop, he sneezed three times as usual. There was always plenty of dust in the shop—dust of ebony, of ivory, of mother-of-pearl, dust of maple and pine and rosewood—of everything, in fact, used in making musical instruments. It floated like gold in the June sunlight.

Perhaps, Oliver thought between sneezes, there's really gold in it. After all there was sometimes gold with jewels set in it on the lutes and citterns his father made.

Stephen Barrett looked up from the mermaid he was carving, smiled at his son and said, "Bless you, Oliver! What is it?"

"My mother asks you, sir, whether the case for the cittern you are making for Master Drake is to be lined with the purple velvet or the crimson. She says if it is to be the crimson I must row across the harbor and fetch a piece. She says that since James and I have learned our Latin and Joyce has made a pudding we may all go—if it is to be the crimson, sir."

"And you think crimson would look best?" Stephen Barrett asked.

He looked solemn, sitting there with his crutch beside him

with the sunlight flashing on his knife, but there was a twinkle in his gray eyes as he added, "I think so too and I'd like well to be on the water myself this fine morning."

"Come too, sir," Oliver said eagerly. "Steer for us. James and I will help you into the boat and Joyce shall bring your cushion."

His father shook his head.

"I must finish this lady's scales and have all smooth and shining in case Frankie—Master Drake—should come. With this south wind it might be today," he said.

"Will it be finished?" Oliver asked.

"The mermaid, yes. That's the last scale. But there's still the rose for the sound hole and the polishing. Oh, there's much to do before the strings sing for us but it will be ready by the end of this month as I promised. See, I have even made the label."

It was a strip of parchment which would be glued on the inner side of the back under the sound hole. It read: "Made by Stephen Barrett of Boston, Lincolnshire, England. June, 1575."

Oliver sneezed again—one of the workmen was sweeping the floor, hunting for a pearl he had dropped—and asked, "If Master Drake lands in Boston today while I'm across there, how shall I know him?"

"Why, by his walk, swinging a little even on dry land as if he were on a ship's deck. And by his look, as if he's just seen a Spanish ship out of those wide blue eyes of his and knows already how to take her. His hair curls a little. It's a sort of brownish-gold but there's red-gold in his beard. I dare say his nose is sunburned and he'll be dressed fine but plain, in good English blue cloth, most like. He may be speaking soft but he never quite keeps the sound of a trumpet or the twang of fiddle strings out of his voice. Oh, you'll know Frank—that is, Master Drake—if you see him. But go across now—don't keep your mother waiting."

There was a forest of masts over in Boston Harbor that June morning. Far above them rose the tower of St Botolph's church, Boston Stump, people called it because it had no pointed spire, only a lantern. It could be seen for many miles at sea and from far across the flat country around it. Oliver liked to hear its great booming bell ring out the hours. Once the sexton had let him ring it. He felt as if the rope would carry him up into the tower, but the sexton had held him down.

Of course he was small then, only eight. He would be twelve tomorrow and he had grown so tall that his cousins, the Campion twins, were both shorter. For a time Joyce had been taller than either of the boys and could knock them both down; one at a time, that is. Oliver liked her better now that he was taller and stronger than she. Still when he and James heard people say that Joyce looked like an English rose, they both made rude noises.

James would groan and say, "Well, roses have thorns, so has she. Look out for her—she scratches, bites too."

Oliver secretly liked Joyce's sunshine-colored hair, pink cheeks and greenish-blue eyes. Perhaps Joyce knew this, because she had not scratched or bitten him for a long time.

She was in a good mood and steered well as they left the Barrett wharf and started across the dancing blue water of the harbor. Oliver and James, as they tugged at their oars, both talked about their favorite subject, Master Francis Drake. Joyce had heard it so many times that she did not listen much. She knew all about how the Barretts and the Drakes, two Protestant families, had been chased out of Devonshire by their Catholic neighbors and how they had gone to live side by side in two old ships drawn up on the shore in Kent. She knew how her Uncle Stephen and the Drake boys—there were twelve of

them—had tumbled in and out of boats almost before they could walk, how they could swim like dolphins and smell a change of wind like gulls.

She knew how her Uncle Stephen, who had been learning how to make viols and lutes from his father, had run away to sea with Frank Drake and had sailed with him on voyages to the Spanish Main. She knew too that from the last of these voyages her uncle had come home with his right leg cut off far above the knee. It had been hurt by a Spanish bullet. The surgeon said that the wound was poisoned and he could do nothing, but Master Drake had said in a voice like the crack of a whip, "Go and tie up that bleeding finger over there! And leave me your tools."

He cut off his friend's leg himself, talking gently all the time, and did it so skillfully, Stephen Barrett would say, "that I hardly felt the pain till after all was over and then mostly in the part of my leg that was not there. Even now, when the wind changes at night into the east, I dream I'm on the Spanish Main once more with Frankie—with Master Drake—and I wake with my right foot aching," he would add and then go back cheerfully to his work of carving and polishing.

Stephen Barrett had come back from that voyage with gold in his pockets. He had bought a good stone house and had built the workshop and the wharf. He chose the house because his wife liked to live within sight of Boston Stump. He would have liked to buy Campions' for her. It had belonged to her grandfather but hard times had come and the Campions had lost the manor and its farms and broad fields.

It had been bought by some people named Desmond. They had come from Ireland and were strangers in Boston, a place where strangers were looked at carefully and for a long time before anyone called them friends. The Desmonds were Catholics. So were the Campion twins. They were second cousins whose parents had died of the plague when the twins were babies. The Barretts had taken care of them ever since.

They went often to Campions', sometimes for lessons in Latin with Father Andrew, the priest there, sometimes to hear Mass in the chapel. In the happy days since Queen Elizabeth had been ruling over England neither Protestants nor Catholics trembled for their lives. It was the law that English people must go to the services of the Church of England on Sundays but they might hear Mass privately. The twins often went to the chapel at Campions'. Oliver sometimes went too, hearing in Latin many of the words he heard in English on Sundays.

He went because Campions' was to him, as it was to his mother and Joyce, the most beautiful place in the world. James cared nothing about it. The last thing he wanted was to be a country squire with cattle and sheep and horses on his green fields. He and Oliver both dreamed of far countries beyond the seas, of sailing with Master Drake into secret harbors, of mules loaded with wedges of gold, of ships ballasted with silver. James also dreamed of hanging a necklace of emeralds as big as walnuts around Isabel Desmond's neck. Oliver thought rubies would be better but never said so. The twins both openly admired Isabel and so did Oliver's mother. Isabel's mother was Spanish and Mistress Barrett had a great deal to say about Isabel's Spanish beauty and about her graceful ways. She was a year older than the twins, a few months older than Oliver and was, he thought privately, like a Spanish princess. He said, however, that he did not like her.

Joyce liked her because James did, but the thing Joyce liked best in the world was horses. To spend a day at Campions' and to ride one of Isabel's palfreys was Joyce's idea of perfect happiness.

Their boat was now passing the mouth of the river that flowed past Campions' and into the harbor. Before the boys knew what Joyce was doing, she had steered them into it. Oliver noticed it first because he saw that Joyce had what he called her Campions' look. Her cheeks got pinker and her eyes greener and her mouth twisted into a half smile.

Oliver dug his oars deep into the brown water. After all the tide was rising. It was about as easy to row up the river as across the harbor. The shop where his mother bought Genoa velvet was as near one as the other. Besides he liked to pass Campions'. It was not only beautiful. There was something mysterious about the Desmonds and Oliver liked mystery.

James had been rowing with his eyes shut. He was pretending

that he was at an oar in a pinnace of Master Drake's. It was a black night and before the moon rose they were going to capture a Spanish galleon. Perhaps two. James had not planned just how to do it. He trusted Master Drake to take care of the details. Suddenly he realized that the choppy water of the harbor had become smooth. He opened his eyes and began to tell Joyce what he thought of her steering.

"Horses!" he exclaimed. "Horses! We're going riding, I suppose! Why didn't you stop her, Oliver?"

"She's the Captain," Oliver said. "You and I are only galley slaves. Besides, we'll get there just as fast—if you'll pull your oar, Master Campion."

James grumbled but pulled his oar. They could see Campions' now. It stood a little higher than the river among strangely shaped trees. They knew them all. There was one clipped into the shape of an eagle. Another was an elephant not much bigger than the eagle. There was a knight on horseback and a ship under full sail. Beyond them was a rose garden where the roses showed red and white against the pinkish brick of the walls.

Joyce did not look at the roses or the house with its shining windows and clusters of tall chimneys.

"There's Lady Clare," she gasped, steering almost into the bank.

"Horses!" growled James.

Lady Clare was black. She had a white star on her forehead and one white foot. She was slender and quick. Her mane and tail flowed like dark water over dark stone. Her coat shone like polished ebony. Her eyes were like jewels out of a queen's crown.

This was what Joyce thought.

Oliver was sure Lady Clare would be good to ride. He had

heard the Desmonds' head groom say she was a decent enough little mare with mayhap a drop of Arab blood in her.

To James she was just another horse, an animal that always wanted to go where he didn't. Horses enjoyed starting to jump, then stopping suddenly, pitching you off into a rose-bush. In James's opinion they needed sails and strong steering gear.

As they passed the house Oliver could see several people on the lawn in the shade of the yew trees. Isabel was there, dressed for riding in blue velvet. Oliver's far-sighted blue eyes could see the jewel that pinned the white plume to her hat and the ivory and gold handle of her riding whip. Sir George Desmond's tall black figure leaned against a column with a griffin ramping on it. Sir George usually leaned against whatever was nearest to him. Everything was black about him—clothes, hair, beard, eyes—except the yellowish skin of his face and hands and the yellow-white of his starched ruff. He was not speaking. Indeed he seldom spoke. Beyond a slow courteous "I wish you a good day, faster Barrett," Oliver had never heard him say anything. However, his wife, also in black and about as broad as she was tall, could scold people in Spanish, French and English and she was doing so now in tones easily heard on the river.

"Doughty! Always Doughty!" Oliver heard her say crossly.

Sir George's steward Jonas Oak was always ready to speak for his master. "Sir George wishes... Sir George says... Sir George thinks..." Oak would say, even to Lady Desmond, in his harsh abrupt voice.

Oak was a pasty-faced, heavily built man with small pale gray eyes, one of which usually seemed to be looking past Oliver's left ear. He was dressed in brownish-gray almost the same muddy color as his hair and beard. Stephen Barrett, who liked most people, said Oak was a fat-fisted varlet and that he would not trust him farther than an acorn would fall on a frosty night. Now Oak said something to Lady Desmond and she was suddenly silent.

Isabel saw them and waved. The boys and Joyce waved too, letting the boat drift back close to the wharf. Oak said something to Father Andrew, the priest, and he called to them to come ashore. He was a cheerful red-faced man who taught Latin to Oliver and James and Isabel.

Joyce steered in towards the wharf. The boys would have gone on to Boston but Isabel called their names. They tied up the boat and walked through the clipped yew trees to the garden.

As they came out past a yew clipped like an elephant, Oak was saying in his harsh grating voice to Sir George: "You are not well enough to ride."

"I want Joyce to ride with me," Isabel said to the boys.

"We have to go to Boston to buy some velvet," Oliver said. "My father is making a cittern for Master Drake to give the Queen. The velvet is to line the case."

"Well, I daresay you are old enough to go alone," Isabel said, switching her whip. "I'll leave Joyce at your house. The groom will bring the horse back. My father was going but he's—he's changed his mind."

"He's not feeling well," Lady Desmond added.

Sir George, who looked no more ill than usual, murmured that he had a slight headache.

Joyce asked politely, "Oh, but would not riding cure it?" yet could not help beaming with happiness when Sir George shook his aching head.

"Sir George needs rest," Jonas Oak said and shouted for the groom. As the girls went to the gate to mount their horses, Oak turned to Oliver and said roughly, "What's that you said about Drake? Is that pirate here?"

"He's not a—" Oliver began, but started sneezing.

Father Andrew blessed him, laughed and said smoothly, "Ah, Oak will be having his jest! Sure he knows the Queen sends Captain Drake out on her business and well he does it too. How long will he and his friend Master Doughty be staying?"

"Why," Oliver said, "he has not come yet. And I heard nothing of his friend."

There was an odd silence in the garden.

Sir George broke it by saying fretfully, "Your arm, Oak. I must rest now."

"We must go too, Lady Desmond," Oliver said.

She waved him and James away impatiently with her fan of black ostrich feathers. She spoke to the priest in a low voice that grew louder as they followed the path through the yews. It rose to shrill tones as they reached the wharf.

"You and Oak and your fine schemes," she said. "I told you Doughty would not come."

Oliver wondered what she meant, but as they rowed towards Boston, he thought mostly about what had been made for him in the shop for his birthday tomorrow. It was always a well-kept secret, but he was sure there would be something. When he had stood there sneezing that morning he had noticed that old Pieter from Antwerp had a piece of moth-eaten blanket thrown over something beside him. Whatever it was, Pieter had been rubbing it with his own secret polish that smelled like honey because it had beeswax in it. It made pieces of fiddleback maple look honey colored. He had a rag, dark with polish and powdered rottenstone, in his hand but he was not polishing anything.

Well, tomorrow I'll know, Oliver thought.

In the meantime there was the crimson velvet to get and he must find out if Captain Drake's ship had come.

No, he was told, there was no sign of her.

The speaker, owner of a little fishing smack full of sole and haddock, asked if Oliver knew where Master Drake would sail next. Wherever it was, he added, it would make the King of Spain squirm and teach him that he didn't own the ocean.

He had seen King Philip once in London when they called him King of England, a man as cold as a dead haddock, he said.

"And if it comes to a fight between Frankie Drake and that red-eyed yellow-faced king, I'll stake my whole year's catch on Frankie to win," the fisherman added and began to unload his fish.

CHAPTER 2

MUSIC AT NIGHT

Wʜᴇɴ ᴛʜᴇ tide went out the next morning, it left a wide pool near Stephen Barrett's wharf. At least if you were over twelve years old it looked like a pool. To Oliver Barrett and the Campion twins it was a secret harbor on the Spanish Main. Into it had just sailed an English galleon and she was moving across the greenish water with every sail set. It was her first voyage. Until this morning she had been hidden under an old blanket in the workshop.

The workmen had all cheered as old Pieter lifted the blanket. There she was, the *Joyce Campion* of Boston, masts and spars well polished, gilded carving at her stern, gun ports along her sides. If you opened them, fierce-looking black cannon showed inside and there were guns at the stern and on the forward castle. Her sails were of strong white linen. Bright flags and pennants hung from her rigging.

Oliver had tried to thank them all but he only started sneezing. The workmen had taken it as thanks and cheered some more. Everyone had had some part in making the galleon.

Henry Green had done the carving. Daniel Simeon had gilded it. One of the Frenchmen had made the hull. Pieter had done the polishing. Englishmen had made the guns. Stephen Barrett himself had done the rigging and James had coiled the ropes. Joyce had helped Mistress Barrett make the sails.

"I have a prick on my finger for every stitch," she stated, showing a slightly roughened left forefinger.

That was when Oliver told her he would name the ship the *Joyce Campion*.

Joyce was so pleased that she began to weave figure eights around Oliver and James.

"We'll sail her to Spain and buy some horses," she said, dancing along towards the pool. "Arab horses!"

James groaned: "Horses! Horses!" and Oliver said, "I'll sail her to Nombre de Dios and load her with gold and silver." After all, it was his ship.

"What good would that do? You can't eat gold or ride on silver. The only thing they are good for is to buy what you like best. We'll still have to go to Spain," Joyce said. "I want a black horse like Isabel's. No, a white horse. No, a golden horse with a silver mane."

"Did you ever see such a horse?" James grunted.

"No, I just made it up. It will be beautiful, won't it, Oliver?"

Oliver said it would. This morning anything seemed beautiful and possible.

They found stones and built a Spanish town beside the pool. They sailed towards it by moonlight, then at dawn. They were just getting ready to attack it when they heard voices above them.

There were three men looking down at them. One was Stephen Barrett with his crutches. Another was a stranger, tall,

splendidly dressed in soft white leather and white velvet with carnations embroidered on the velvet. He had a black cloak lined with carnation-colored velvet and a jeweled hat on one side of his black head. He wore jewels in his ears too and on his slender fingers. Joyce noticed them and his long narrow green eyes like pale green emeralds. He had a soft black beard. His chin and upper lip were shaven a little so that his mustache was only a narrow line. It showed his twisting scarlet lips.

Joyce hated him at once.

The boys saw none of these things. They were looking at the third man. There he was in his plain dark blue clothes, just as Stephen Barrett had said, smiling down at them out of those very wide, very blue eyes, with the sunshine making his beard like red gold. Yes, and his nose was already sunburned and peeling a little. No doubt it was Master Drake.

They climbed up the bank. The boys made their best bows and Joyce her curtsy. It is hard to curtsy gracefully in a high wind that has blown your hair round your eyes, with a skirt wet around the bottom and with muddy feet. Still, Joyce did very well, Oliver thought.

Master Drake only smiled at them without speaking but Oliver already felt as if they knew each other. Master Drake's friend was more talkative.

"And what, my little lad, is your name?" he asked sweetly, in a voice like an alto recorder.

He laid his hand on Oliver's head.

Oliver hated being called a lad. Only a few minutes before he had been captain of his own ship. He wriggled out from under the jeweled hand, muttering that his name was Oliver Barrett.

"This is Master Thomas Doughty," Master Drake said in a soft voice that still had the tone of a trumpet in it.

Master Doughty called James a lad too but James ducked in time so that no hand was placed on his head. Then it was Joyce's turn.

"And this little lady?" Master Doughty said, smoothing her hair away from her hot pink cheeks.

"I'm no lady," Joyce said and bit him.

Oliver could not help admiring Master Doughty's self-control.

He made no sound and he smiled pleasantly while he looked at the half circle of tooth marks on the edge of his hand.

To Stephen Barrett's embarrassed apology he only said gently, "Luckily there is little blood drawn."

He took a small flask of ruby and gold glass from his white leather pouch and put a few drops of whatever was in it, something that smelled like roses and spice, on his wound and wrapped his hand in his silk handkerchief.

Stephen Barrett said to Joyce, "Run along to your aunt now, Joyce."

Mistress Barrett was really the twins' second cousin once removed, but Aunt was a more convenient title.

"Tell her," Stephen Barrett added, "that Master Drake and Master Doughty will dine with us and sleep here tonight." Then he said to the boys, "Master Drake has sent his man back across the harbor for their cloak-bags. Wait here till the boat comes and help carry the things to the house. In the meantime we'll visit the shop."

He started swinging slowly along on his crutches towards the workshop. Master Doughty walked beside him, talking all the time, offering his arm, hoping the little lady would not be punished—it was nothing, nothing at all—praising everything. He spoke well of Boston Stump. The tower would be handsome when it was finished, he said. Hearing that Boston people considered it finished, he added hastily that it had a look of massive strength. He also praised Barretts' Cove, saying that it must be a lovesome spot when the tide was in and the mudflats covered. He said that the Campions were handsome children—if you liked that red-blond English type so apt to look like underdone roast beef later. He himself thought Master Barrett's son far handsomer. Irish, quite Irish, with those very deep blue eyes and the black hair. What, only twelve today? A fine tall lad. About twelve, boys often started falling over their feet but they outgrew it after a time.

Master Doughty's voice died away and Oliver did not hear any more compliments.

Master Drake said, "Tell me who built your galleon."

They told him while he held it in his hand, and how the town they had built was Nombre de Dios and they had just been going to seize it when he came.

Drake said, "So you know about Nombre de Dios, do you?"

"My father tells us stories at night by the fire sometimes. We like that one best," Oliver said.

"I wish I may have a ship as good as your galleon next time I sail the Spanish Main—or anywhere else," Master Drake said. "Now I must go and see her makers."

He handed back the *Joyce Campion* and swung off towards the shop with that seaman's roll in his gait.

"We must go with him," Oliver said.

"To the shop?" asked James.

"No. Wherever he's going. To the end of the world."

The boat came soon. They carried the cloak-bags—Master Drake's small one, Master Doughty's three large ones—to the house. There was a great bustle in the steaming kitchen. Oliver could smell salmon boiling and spring lamb roasting before the fire. He could also smell his mother's best currant spice cake baking. Joyce, looking neat, clean, and downcast, was shelling the first peas of the season. Eggs were being beaten, silver spoons polished, mint crushed for mint sauce to go with the lamb.

Mistress Barrett finished filling the gilt salt cellar, the one like a shell held up by a dolphin, and set it on the table.

"Now," she said briskly, "do put on your best clothes, for you shall wait on Master Drake and his friend, such a fine gentleman, that Master Doughty! He'll be a great help to Master Drake, I promise you, presenting him to great folk at court, such as Master Christopher Hatton whose secretary he is. Then my Lord Burghley himself offered him—but that's a secret—well, what are you waiting for? Your green doublet, James. Your blue one, Oliver. Be sure your hands are clean, scrub them well in the scullery. Now, don't go spilling water on Master Doughty when you bring the bowl and ewer after the lamb is eaten. Hand the napkins as I have always shown you, not thrusting them into their faces. I wish I had taught you to serve kneeling but it's too late now, but mind you, bow low as you bring the dishes, especially to Master Doughty."

At this point Joyce groaned.

"And that will be enough from you, miss. Eleven years old, almost twelve, and from a family better than any Drakes, I promise you. You'll soon be thirteen. Girls are married at thirteen. I was a bride myself at fourteen. If your uncle—and Master Doughty—had not begged my patience to you this day, you'd be shut in your room without bite or sup, I vow."

Oliver murmured, "Without bite, anyway."

Luckily his mother did not hear him but went on giving instructions to everyone within sound of her voice.

All went well. The dinner was perfection. Master Doughty said so and of course he must know. He had been in Italy and he swore that Mistress Barrett's flummery was as good as a favorite Italian dish of his, if he could just have a grating of nutmeg—if it's no trouble.

Master Drake ate heartily and said little. Evidently he liked to hear Master Doughty talk. So did everyone below the salt— the maids, the shopmen and Maria, Oliver's old nurse. After Master Drake had eaten, he went back to the shop again with Stephen Barrett. Master Doughty held the maids and Mistress Barrett spellbound with his talk of Italy and France. The children, though still hungry, tagged along after Master Drake.

They went to look at the cittern again after supper. Master Doughty compared it to instruments he had seen in Italy. He was surprised to find such work in England. The Queen had a lute something like it only with two mermaids on the back. Still the back of this lute—or cittern, if you call it so—carved like a shell, is very well, very well indeed.

Master Drake said less but thought more, Oliver decided, about the cittern as well as about everything else. The only thing that seemed to trouble Drake about the cittern was getting it to the Queen.

"By the time it is finished, Stephen," he said, "I must be in Plymouth and the Queen will be at Kenilworth in Warwickshire where she is to visit my Lord Leicester on her summer's progress. I hope to be busy with affairs more important than even the finest cittern in the world, which no doubt this will be. Can you send it into Warwickshire, Stephen?"

"Yes, I can. John Bodkin is a trusty man and he's from Warwickshire. He'll know the roads. I'll send him."

Master Drake said, "I saw him at dinner, I think. Short, sturdy, like the stump of an old oak? Looks as if he drank vinegar instead of beer? Send him by all means, but send the boys too. The Queen likes well-mannered boys who sing and thrum on citterns."

James and Oliver stared at him with their mouths open. It could not really be true. But it was. Master Doughty approved and gave them much good advice which Oliver barely heard. He did hear his father say, "They seem rather young," and Master Drake laugh and answer, "Why, Stephen, you and I were both at sea in a leaky old bark when we were no older! Learning the Dutch coast, remember? And my young cousin, John Drake, named for my brother, goes with me on my next voyage."

"To the end of the world, perhaps," Master Doughty put in.

"It may be only to Morocco," Master Drake said, frowning a little. "But John, who goes with me, is but little older than your son."

"I'll make all right with the lad's mother," Master Doughty said. "After the music. When she's rested from her cares, that will be the time."

Oliver thought afterwards that the music that evening was the best ever heard in the Barretts' kitchen. James had never sung better in the madrigals. Oliver knew by the way his father looked at him that he himself had played his viol well, and later on the cittern. But anyone who had a tune running always in his head and whose fingers were not all thumbs could play the cittern. The tune in Oliver's head just now was "Greensleeves" and his fingers seemed to find the chords themselves. Outside in an apple tree a blackbird was singing while he played. He wondered, yawning, if the blackbird had the air of "Greens-leeves" running in his head too. And the nightingales? As the moon came up behind Boston Stump they began singing too and Oliver never knew when they stopped.

Chapter 3

KENILWORTH

IT WAS Master Drake himself who had carried Oliver to bed, his mother told him. He made nothing of the weight. Master Doughty had carried James. Joyce had walked by herself though half asleep and would have no help, silly girl. Yes, they had sailed already, wind and tide serving. John Bodkin had set them across the harbor. Now it was time for the boys to go to Campions' for their Latin lesson.

"None of those noises!" Mistress Barrett added sharply. "Master Drake himself wishes he had the Latin but has not, going to sea so early. The Queen speaks Latin. Let them speak a piece of it when they hand her the cittern, he says. 'Write something for them to say, Tom,' he says to Master Doughty and he's written it. Now where did I put it? In the sugar basin? Under the pewter platter? Well, I'll find it. Go on now to Father Andrew. Have you both got clean handkerchiefs? Well, behave as well as you look and I'll warrant the Queen will be pleased with you but you've weeks to get more Latin, and some Greek would be good to have too, Master Doughty says. Slip along now. Come, Joyce, we'll make a meat pasty for dinner."

So it was true—they were going to carry the cittern to the Queen.

"And then," James said, "she'll send us to the Spanish Main with Master Drake and when we come back our pockets will be lined with gold and I'll buy myself a galleon and sail right round the world."

Oliver had plans too. He was in India one minute, discovered a Northwest Passage around America the next and then dashed across the Channel to Dunkirk and rescued a beautiful Huguenot girl right under the nose of King Philip of Spain. She looked like Isabel.

Father Andrew found them unusually stupid that morning. He boxed Oliver's ears, gave James's arm a sharp twist and sent them home with extra-long tasks for the next day. He also whipped them a little around the legs with Isabel's gold-handled riding whip which happened to be handy.

Isabel was waiting for them near the clipped yews as they came out into the sunshine shaking themselves.

"So you were whipped again!" she said.

The boys said nothing.

Isabel, Oliver thought, might look a little like the girl he had rescued from Dunkirk but she really was nothing like her. For one thing the Huguenot girl had admired his courage and had tied up his wounded arm with her own scarf.

"Will you never learn?" Isabel asked. "The sentences were easy enough. I got mine all right."

Altogether this was a bad morning. They went swimming on the way home in a favorite pool and were late to dinner and were both whipped again. However, Stephen Barrett did not really enjoy whipping people and by evening they had forgotten all about it.

There was no music after supper that night. Instead Stephen Barrett told of his voyages with Drake, and particularly of Nombre de Dios, from which expedition he had returned laden with Spanish gold. It was a bright evening. The shopmen brought bits of work that could be done quietly, fine carving or polishing or gilding. The women sewed. Stephen Barrett himself worked on the mermaid's tail as he talked. The boys whittled out spars for a pinnace to sail with the *Joyce Campion*.

The cittern was finished in time.

"It is the most beautiful one in the world," Oliver said.

Stephen Barrett laughed. "You've seen all the others, then?"

Oliver said sturdily, "If the Queen does not say so I'll eat all the velvet left from lining the case."

"I'll tell your mother to save the scraps," Stephen Barrett said smiling. "Come, tune it, Oliver, and play, and James will sing for us."

So James sang old songs—"Bonny Lass upon a Green" and "Phyllis on the New Mown Hay" and Oliver set the strings of the cittern singing too.

"It needs playing," Stephen Barrett said. "You must play it every day so it will be in good voice."

It was in good voice when they started on their journey into Warwickshire. Master Drake had written to tell them that the Queen would come to the Earl of Leicester's castle of Kenilworth on July 9th.

Be there on that morning [he wrote]. Seek out Master Robert Laneham, Keeper of the Council Door. He is a servant of the Earl's as well as of the Queen's. He will find out from Lord Leicester when you may best carry the cittern to Her Majesty. Laneham will advise you what to do. He is none of your rough sailor men such as F. Drake, but knows courtly manners. Master Doughty has wrote some Latin verses for you to speak. There is some Greek in them too, I think. My poor head makes little of them but they are very fine, no doubt, and to the Queen's taste. I am not more afraid of powder and shot than are most men, I think, nor of hurricanes at sea, but my knees would shake if I needs must say Greek to a Queen, I promise you. So, if yours do, it might be well to hand the paper for her to read. Master Doughty has wrote it out in a fine Italian hand. Play and sing for her some old English song such as "Since First I Saw Your Face." Make sure the cittern is in tune and does not twang like an old frog on a hot night.

I left gold with your father for your journey. I wish you fine weather, a good journey, a good return. Write to me, if you will, how Her Grace likes the cittern.

Yours,

F. Drake

Master Doughty had written not only Latin verses but much advice on manners, on the brushing of hair, the cleaning of fingernails, the care of stockings when kneeling (always choose a clean dry spot yet do not appear to choose it). He also gave helpful hints about eating in courtly fashion. (When a dish of cakes is offered, do not touch one and put it back. Quickly choose the largest and let the dish pass on.)

He said that while the Queen was at table many dishes would be offered, two hundred, three hundred. The Queen would eat little or none and it is uncourteous to load your plate when she is present. When she leaves you will have a chance, if you act quickly, to get the best bits for yourself.

"Do not come near Her Grace after riding until you have changed your clothes and washed yourselves well. Better use some scent. Her Majesty has a keen nose and is offended when men smell like stable boys."

"If he had only left some of his sweet-smelling perfume!" Mistress Barrett said.

"He has," Stephen Barrett said. "The letter reeks of it."

"If he sent any, I'd rub Brown Bouncer down with it," Oliver said.

"You'll treat no honest horse so!" Joyce said fiercely.

"No," said Oliver, "I'll not and I'll wash with soap and water. What else does he say?"

"He thinks you should both wear suits of white velvet with long gowns of violet silk over them. He says he saw the Queen listen most graciously to a child who played the lute dressed thus. He also had a scarf of white and silver wrapped around his head like a Turk's turban."

"Joyce and I could easily make turbans," Mistress Barrett said eagerly. "I've an old dress I could cut up and with plumes of peacock's feathers—"

Joyce groaned. So did the boys.

"He kindly says this is not necessary," Stephen Barrett added.

So when the boys started on their journey, they carried the cittern in its case of fine English leather and in their cloak-bags were their best suits of Lincoln wool.

"I daresay the Queen will like you in good English cloth

as well as she would in foreign velvet," Stephen Barrett said. "She'd better," said Joyce, but Mistress Barrett still wished they could be dressed like Turks.

It was fortunate that John Bodkin knew Warwickshire. The third day they found the highways so crowded that they could hardly move. Every man, woman and child in central England seemed to be headed for Kenilworth Castle. Many rode, but more trudged through the dust under the hot July sun. Every crossroad brought in new crowds of people. They had to make way for droves of oxen, herds of swine, flocks of sheep, all to be roasted that week. There were carts loaded with game or fruit for the castle, couriers riding fast and shouting, "Make way, make way for the Queen's service," riders hurrying with fresh salmon, carts with barrels of oysters, carts full of flowers. There were splendidly dressed gentlemen on prancing horses, noble ladies carried in gilded chairs, Morris dancers, tumblers, musicians, players with hobby-horses.

John Bodkin knew where the narrow lanes led. Some times they slipped down one that was hardly more than a tunnel between hedges full of briar roses in bloom. They would leave one crowded highway and come back into another as crowded and as dusty. Sometimes a lucky family turned off the high road because they had reached the farm of a friend where they would find food and lodging. In the villages every inn was already so crowded that there was no room to sleep even on the hay in the stables.

Oliver and James were lucky. John Bodkin brought them to his cousin's farm. Dame Bodkin led them to a clean little room with dark beams so low that they could reach up and touch them. There was a mattress full of clean straw on the floor and on top of it one of goose feathers.

"From the very geese that tried to chase you out of the farm-yard just now," jolly Dame Bodkin told them. "Have you seen Kenilworth yet? Well, look out of your window."

They fell over each other to reach it. There rose the towers. One was so old they called it Caesar's Tower, Dame Bodkin said. Others had been built during many centuries. The Earl of Leicester himself had added a building in the newest shape with mullioned windows. Yes, that part where the sun flashes so bright on the glass. Most wonderful to the boys was the clock on Caesar's Tower. Its face was painted the blue of the summer sky so that its golden hands and numbers seemed to be floating in the air.

"There's another face like it looking south," Dame Bodkin said. "They do say that when the Queen comes, God bless every step she takes with her pretty little feet, the hands on both sides will be stopped and the bell that rings the hours will be silent so that time will stand still while she is here. They say she'll enter the castle by the new bridge across the lake. Look—lean out—you'll see just a bit of it among the trees. Master Bodkin helped cut timber for it. It's so long you won't believe it, and sanded as clean as my kitchen floor for Her Majesty to ride across. And there's heathen gods on it such as Neptune with fish and Ceres with grain and what all I don't know and you'll see for yourselves. Oh, there'll be fine doings there.

"The men of Coventry are going to give their play of the Danes and Saxons there and more than one will splash into the water, no doubt. And if you want to wash, young masters, there's water in the well and an oaken bucket to carry it to the scullery and soap made sweet with my own lavender. Hurry now, for they say she will come at two o'clock and I for one will be on the road to see her."

Master Drake had sent with his own letter one for Master Laneham. With John Bodkin as their guide they hurried to the castle gate to be there before two. The hands of the clock in the sky moved past two. At the gate they learned that so many people had thronged to see the Queen that she would be late in reaching the castle. The guards at the gate knew John Bodkin and they knew Master Laneham too. He would be in the Queen's train, one of the guards told them. The Queen would hold council with her ministers as in London and Laneham would keep the council door. There was no use trying to see him today.

Oliver showed him the letter Master Drake had written to Master Laneham. The guard showed it to his fellow guard.

"Look here, Dickon," he said, "here's a letter from Master Drake to Master Laneham asking him to admit these young gentlemen and John Bodkin to the park and courtyard. It's wrote with his own hand. It's that Drake that kicked harder than King Philip's mules at Nombre de Dios. Shall I let them pass?"

Dickon said, "From Master Drake, eh?" and waved them in.

They saw the finely sanded bridge with the statues on it but they could not get close enough to see what they were. They saw an island near the lake shore that suddenly began to move and float towards them. They ricked their necks gazing up at the clock. The hands still moved at three, at four, at five o'clock. By six a great crowd had gathered around the lake.

Oliver heard a man in the crowd say that the Earl had met the Queen seven miles away.

"Yes," said another, "and he's had a tent like a palace set up where she can rest."

"How big is it?" Oliver asked.

"Why, that's hard to tell, young master, though I helped set it up myself. But I'll say this—it took seven carts just to carry the tent pegs. There's rooms and rooms with tapestries on the walls and carpets laid over the green grass. Almost before we had it set up, they were decking a dining table with fine linen and glass and gold dishes, and the cooks were bawling at the scullions."

Oliver said, "But why doesn't she come?"

"Oh, there's the feasting and then hunting the red deer through the forest. They'll be shooting from the backs of their horses as they go. I've heard the hunters' horns this last hour. Watch the curve of the road there below us. When the people clear the way and line the sides, it will mean she's coming. Hark! Do you not hear trumpets?"

The hands of the clock on Caesar's Tower had almost reached eight when at last they saw that people were moving to the sides of the road. Then the trumpets blew and they saw the procession, small spots of bright color with golden dust rising around them. Suddenly shouts were louder than trumpets and they knew that the figure on the white horse must be the Queen.

She vanished among the trees but the shouting kept coming closer. The hands of the clock in the sky reached eight and stopped. No bell struck the hour. On the floating island in the shadowy lake torches were starting to flare. The island moved in its mysterious way towards the bridge. Silence fell on the people around them and all eyes were fixed on the road to the bridge. The trumpets were quite close now.

"Here come the Earl's men," said Bodkin. "See the banner— that's his device: the bear and the ragged staff."

Lord Leicester's men lined up along the bridge: trumpeters, heralds, men at arms. Then came knights and ladies richly dressed. Mist was rising from the lake and through it twilight and torchlight shone on green and silver or scarlet and gold. There were scattered cheers as the crowd recognized familiar figures, and the cheers deepened as Lord Leicester, tall and handsome, carrying the Queen's sceptre, appeared. Then silence, or not quite silence, rather a soft sigh of delight as the crowd drew breath. At last she came in sight on her white horse and the shouts were like roaring lions, like thunder, like falling mountains as she passed.

Oliver was too far away to see her face. All he could see was that she was in purple and gold with a plumed hat, and that her horse with its rich trappings seemed part of her.

Why, she rides even better than Isabel, he thought.

The Queen stopped at the center of the bridge and the floating island, brightly blazing with torches now. On it a tall lady, who said she was the Lady of the Lake, proclaimed: "The Lake, the Lodge, the Lord are yours now to command."

He could hear the Queen laugh and reply that she had supposed the domain was hers already but nonetheless she thanked the lady for her courtesy. Then she rode on to the castle gate. Here she was stopped by an enormous porter, a giant eight feet tall with a great rough club and keys a foot long.

"I know not what all this riding and trudging about is," he roared. "Such a noise never I heard. At first I could not tell the reason for it. But now at last I find myself pierced by a personage of such heroic sovereignty that it calms my wonder."

Then he knelt and prayed for pardon for such ignorance. The Queen laughed and granted him pardon and he gave up his club and keys and ordered the trumpeters to sound a welcome.

John Bodkin said, "Those trumpeters are all near eight foot tall. Ah, we have giants in Warwickshire! Their silver trumpets are five foot long and they blow them as easily as you would a penny whistle, Master Oliver."

There was music from oboes and comets as the Queen rode into the torchlit courtyard. They could see her dismount and walk across to the palace, now shining with waxlights from every window. The trumpeters were at the door. She looked very small as she vanished through it.

CHAPTER 4

CASTLE GARDEN

THEY STUMBLED home more asleep than awake and they slept until Dame Bodkin called them to go to church. It was at the church that they saw Master Laneham. John Bodkin pointed him out, standing on the steps of the church, bowing briskly to a richly dressed lady.

"Aye, that's Bob himself; Master Laneham, I suppose I must say now, though we were whipped by the same school master and we fed hay to the same horses. He's a great man now by the Earl's favor. Aye, that's the one, with the biggest, stiffest ruff in the churchyard."

Master Laneham was a quick-moving, sharp-eyed, sharp nosed, rosy-faced man. He was dressed in black velvet with satin slashings the same color as his cheeks. His black velvet bonnet had a big plume of shining cock's feathers and his ruff was certainly the widest and starchiest anywhere in sight.

"His face looks like a strawberry on a platter," Oliver said.

John Bodkin never laughed, but he did smile occasionally and he did so now.

However, he quickly put on his usual sober face and said, "Do you be respectful to him now, Master Oliver, or you'll not see the Queen."

"Shall we speak to him now?" Oliver asked.

"Not till after church. We'll sit at the back and see him when he comes out. He'll be up in front with the great folk. We used to call him the Black Prince when we were boys," John Bodkin added.

"Why?" Oliver asked.

"Oh, he had black hair and those bright black eyes and then he had a way of sitting a horse and giving orders to the rest of us that made us mock him with the name. Yet we looked up to him in a way, even after we'd just doused him in the horse trough. But there, he's gone in and we must go too."

Oliver could see Master Laneham during the service and hear his voice above others, singing the chants. He sang well, Oliver thought, but no better than James. He was proud of James and wished he could sing like that himself. He had no voice except one in his head, and to make that sound he needed his viol or a cittern.

He was close to the church steps with John Bodkin when Master Laneham came out. Laneham's sharp eyes lighted on John Bodkin and he greeted him kindly.

As a prince would a stable boy, Oliver thought.

"Why, how come you here, my good John?" Master Laneham said. "I thought you lived in the shadow of Boston Stump. But then, all come our way today. You have prospered, I see, and glad of it I am. But what can I do for you, Honest John?"

John smiled his vinegary smile for the second time that day. Oliver wondered if he was thinking of the horse trough.

"Why, Prince—that is Master Laneham—I've brought my

master's son, Oliver Barrett, and James Campion, his cousin. They bear a letter for you from Master Francis Drake. Master Oliver has it here."

"Ah yes! We know Master Drake and will read his letter," said Master Laneham still in his princely way.

He read the letter, his sharp black eyes glancing fast along the lines, and then said, snapping his fingers, "Now I must speak to my lord about this. These are busy days as you well may guess, John, but on Master Drake's account we must slip these lads in, especially since they are musicians. We have a weakness for music."

"I heard you singing," Oliver said, "it sounded fine."

"And I heard your cousin and I say the same," Master Laneham said with his brisk bow. "Now let us cogitate. This afternoon there is dancing and in the evening fireworks over the lake. Monday there's a grand hunt and we can never tell when that may end. Tuesday there is no great thing planned, just music in the garden and that not till the edge of evening. Yes, we'll try Tuesday. I will speak to my Lord Leicester. Come to the gate of Mortimer's Tower and ask for me. Wait, I will write you a pass."

He had an inkhorn and quill at his belt, slips of parchment in his pouch. Using an old stump as a desk he wrote: "Admit J. Bodkin and musicians O. Barrett, J. Campion to Kenilworth Castle, Tuesday, 13th July, 1575," and signed it R. Laneham.

"You can see the fireworks from the shore of the lake tonight," he said, waved their thanks aside, and was soon making one of his swift bows to a lady in purple velvet.

"It would have given me much pleasure to dine in your company, but alas I must to my lord. Busy day, busy days!" he said and in a moment was on the back of his quick stepping black horse and riding off towards Kenilworth.

They saw the fireworks that night, blazing darts, flashing stars, serpents like lightning. Sometimes the great banners that floated from all the castle towers would be lost in smoke clouds. Sometimes a blaze of fire would show Lord Leicester's bear and ragged staff or Queen Elizabeth's Tudor roses or her lions and lilies.

Sky and water both seemed on fire. The noise of exploding rockets echoed across the lake and the shouts of the onlookers seemed to follow them up into the sky.

"I shall hear thunder all night," said Oliver as he was getting into bed, and was asleep almost before he said it.

The next day he practiced on the cittern and James sang with him. When they stopped to rest they could hear hunting horns sounding through the forest. Once, at the foot of a green hill across the fields, they saw hunters gathered, waiting quietly. Then they heard hounds baying and yelping. A stag went bounding past and the hunters galloped after him. Dame Bodkin said that the figure in crimson on the black horse was the Queen.

Since the horse looked no bigger than a cricket, Oliver wondered how she could tell.

"I saw her this morning, Queen Elizabeth herself, God bless her, as close as I am to you," Dame Bodkin said. "Oh, the plumes and the jewels and the crimson velvet, it was a fair treat, and how she can ride! Once her horse is frightened and up he bounds into the air, but the Queen reins him in and calms him. To those gentlemen who sprang to the bridle she cries out, 'No hurt! No hurt!' which was the best thing we heard all day, I swear."

At last it was Tuesday, their great day and a fine hot sunny one. They swam in the brook nearby and scrubbed themselves with Dame Bodkin's soap. When they were dressed in their best suits she inspected them and said, "Well, you'll pass in a crowd." She reminded Oliver of his mother and he decided they must look all right. John Bodkin had twisted his ankle the day before, climbing up a steep bank to try to see the hunt go by. They knew their way now so he did not need to go with them.

Dame Bodkin said, "Now, don't fear the Queen's Grace. No matter how fine she goes in velvet with jewels as big as pullets' eggs, she is a friend to her people, the best friend we have. Now get along with you, find Master Laneham and you'll soon see her."

But Master Laneham was not to be found.

"He's gone on an errand for his lordship," the giant porter told them at the gate of Mortimer's Tower. "To find musicians to sit inside a dolphin, he said. Ah, these are strange days at Kenilworth. I don't know what we're coming to. You might try the garden—he went that way."

"Let's go and play leapfrog there," James suggested.

"Carrying the cittern while we do it, I suppose," Oliver said. "We have to find Master Laneham and then the Queen."

The cittern in its leather case was getting heavier every minute.

"We might find the Queen in the garden," James said. "I hear ladies' voices—unless they are peacocks."

There were peacocks but there were also splendidly dressed ladies, laughing and talking as they strolled along the finely sanded paths among the red and white roses.

Oliver thought, Which one is the Queen? Which hand do I hold the cittern in? Which hand do I take off my cap with? Where did I put Master Drake's letter? And Master Doughty's poem? How did it go? Elizabeth Regina gloriosa—no, that's not right. Where shall I kneel?

"Where is she?" he said aloud, shifting the cittern from his left hand to his right and wiping his face with his handkerchief.

"She isn't here," said James. "No one has a crown or a sceptre. Let's go and look at the fountain."

There were many streams coming from the fountain. The wind whisked the drops through the air, sprinkling the marble statues that stood among the clipped yews.

"They ought to have a fountain at Campions'," James said. "I wish Isabel could see this one."

Above the fountain was Lord Leicester's bear with the ragged staff carved in white marble. On one side was Neptune with his spear, ready to spear the fish that swam in the cool water of the pool. On the other a nymph rode on a dolphin.

At one end of the garden they saw a great bird cage with its wires fastened to columns with jeweled tops. At least the jewels looked like real emeralds and rubies and pearls until the boys stood quite close and saw that they were only painted.

"The birds look painted too," Oliver said. He pointed to a rainbow-colored macaw climbing the wires and added, "I'll bring one home like him for Isabel, a green one."

"Where from?" asked James and added quickly, "so will I. A pink and gray one."

"Why, from wherever we go when we sail with Master Drake."

A red and green parrot repeated, "With Master Drake!"

James jumped but Oliver only said calmly, "See—even the birds know, but he'll never take us if we don't find the Queen and give her the cittern."

"Well, let's ask that lady over there, the one in the arbor reading."

The lady looked cool and comfortable in the green shade of the arbor. She wore a white dress and her face and hands were almost as white as her dress. She had a net of silver sewn with pearls over her reddish-gold hair. The eyes she raised from her book were sea-blue, Oliver saw.

"Well, what is it, young masters?" she said.

Oliver made his best bow. "Please, my lady," he began.

Then something terrible happened. He sneezed—three times.

"Bless you," the lady said after the third sneeze. "You were saying?"

"Could you tell us where we can find the Queen? We have a present for her from Master Francis Drake, and a letter."

"Have you never seen the Queen?" the lady asked. "I thought she was in the garden."

"We saw her, but only a long way off," James said. "It was the day the clock stood still. We saw her ride across the bridge. She was all shining with jewels, like the bird cage. I could see the torchlight flashing on them."

"And did you see her?" the lady asked Oliver.

"Not her face," Oliver said. "But I saw her walking after she got off her horse. I'd know her by her walk. It's as if she heard music even when it's not playing. And she has tiny little feet," he added. "I think one would fit in my hand."

"I'll tell her what you say," the lady said. "Will you tell me your names?"

"I am Oliver Barrett from Boston in Lincolnshire where my father makes musical instruments and this is my cousin, James Campion."

"Campion? I thought that was a West Country name. There were Campions of the old religion somewhere in the West, I think."

"They are distant cousins, my aunt told me," James said. "I am of the old religion too, my lady, and so is Joyce, that's my sister, but not Oliver or his father and mother."

"And you are happy together? No quarrels? No harsh words? No long faces?"

"Joyce and James and I quarrel sometimes because she only likes horses and we like the sea. We want to sail with Master Drake and bring back gold for the Queen," Oliver said.

"None for yourselves?"

"Oh yes, for ourselves too. James wants to buy a ship and fight the Spanish. I'll buy a manor Joyce wants and a horse. We disagree about the color of horses but we don't quarrel about religion. We all go to church at Boston Stump and sometimes I go with my mother to hear Mass in the chapel. She says that religion ought to make friends, not enemies."

"And she is right," said the lady, shutting her book sharply. "If God is worshipped in the name of Jesus Christ it matters not if the words be Latin or English. It is not our pleasure," she said, "that our people should hate and slay and burn each other, that Spaniards or French should steal our country in the name of religion."

There was something in her voice that made Oliver kneel down in front of her and say to his cousin, "Kneel, James, kneel down. It is the Queen's Grace."

James said, "Forgive us, Your Highness, for not knowing," and was on his knees on the grass.

The wind blew drops from the fountain over them and must have blown some on the Queen's pale face too because she wiped them off with a handkerchief like a cobweb and said, "Now, come, let me see my lute."

"It's more of a cittern really," Oliver said and handed her the case and Master Drake's letter.

The Queen said, "You may stand up. Now what will they

say to you at home for getting grass green on the knees of your best stockings?"

"That the stain came there in the best cause of any we ever got," said Oliver. Whenever Oliver thought of Kenilworth, on nights of stinging frost on some far-off sea, this was the hour he remembered. He would see again the hot sun making rainbows in the fountain, feel the cool of long shadows on the grass, breathe the scent of roses, taste a strawberry sweet on his tongue. Music from the cittern would slip out from his fingers and James's voice would soar up into the blue like a skylark. He would hear the Queen herself try the strings and hear her say, "Why, it sounds as well as it looks! You say it's not a lute? More of a cittern really? Well, I vow, it's the finest cittern in the world and will tell Master Drake so."

She missed none of its beauties. She noticed every scale of the mermaid's tail, the pegs carved like the lilies of her coat armor, and the inlaid lilies of mother-of-pearl. She praised the Tudor Rose of emeralds, rubies and pearls over the sound hole and the delicate carving of sandalwood on which it rested.

The neck ended in a carved ivory head wearing a gold crown. She liked that too. Her ladies gathered round listening to the music, first in happy silence, then chattering again as the Queen showed them the cittern. At last she rose from her seat and handed it to one of them, telling her to put it in the safest place in the castle.

Oliver suddenly thought of Master Doughty's poem.

"There were some verses I was to say, in Latin and also in Greek, some very fine things about Your Majesty. The poem is by Master Thomas Doughty."

"Can you remember it?" asked the Queen.

"No, Your Grace," Oliver replied truthfully.

"Good," said the Queen. "It seems everyone in England can write verses. I believe half Warwickshire will spout Latin to me this week. Let today be a holiday."

So the letter from Master Drake and Master Doughty's poem were put into the case with the cittern and the boys walked beside the Queen as she strolled through the garden, ordering them to pick strawberries or cherries for her and then telling them to eat them for her too. She walked over the bridge and a little way into the park, her ladies following.

During the walk she said to the boys, "Now, how shall I repay you for your long journey?"

Oliver said, "Why, we are already repaid, Your Grace."

"Shall I not ask Lord Leicester to let you help his servants to make music some evening?"

The boys stammered out their thanks and she added, "But that is for my pleasure—what for yours?"

"If Your Majesty pleases, let us sail with Master Drake," Oliver said.

He had turned very pink and his dark curls were pushed up all over his head in a way that would have made Mistress Barrett, Dame Bodkin and any maiden aunt reach for the brush.

The Queen laughed good naturedly.

"Master Drake? Is he going somewhere?" she asked. "Well, when I thank him for the cittern, which is the fairest ever I saw, I shall tell him you did your errand well. And I'll tell no one you did not know Master Doughty's Latin," she added. "Here, you may have my hand to kiss and now be off with you."

She was gone before they were off their knees. They stood looking after her as she crossed the bridge, as majestic in her simple white dress as if she wore a crown and carried a sceptre, as if all the trumpets were blowing.

CHAPTER 5

PAVANE

THE NEXT day Master Laneham rode up to Bodkin farm, picked his way daintily across the farmyard and told Oliver and James to come quickly to Kenilworth.

"Master Goldingham needs you," he said.

Of course they knew about Master Goldingham. He wrote verses for nymphs to say as they stepped out of holly bushes, for comic porters and wild men of the woods. He also wrote plays and drilled musicians.

"But how did he know about us?" James asked.

"Mayhap the Queen's Grace told him," Master Laneham said.

He told them to go to a house in the Park near the lake where the musicians were rehearsing. He even told them how to knock at the music-room door.

"It is uncivil," he said, "to knock more than once. At the door of a bedchamber you should scratch with your fingernails but at the music room you may knock but not like a blacksmith beating out a horseshoe. Wait till the music stops. Knock firmly but gently. If no one comes, try the door. If it be locked do not fiddle with the lock, nor peek through the keyhole. Retire till the music ceases again, then try once more. If asked your name, give your last name only.

"You mean we are not to say this is Lord James Campion and Marquis Oliver Barrett?" Oliver asked.

"Not unless you would like Master Goldingham to eat you alive," Master Laneham said with a snap of his black eyes.

He told them that there would be six players of viols and as many singers inside a twenty-four-foot dolphin. Arion, whose part would be taken by a fine singer called Harry Golding, would ride outside. Inside the players of the viols and the singers would accompany him.

"Now," Master Laneham said, "my lord desires each note so clearly sung, each instrument so cleanly touched and excellently tuned that the whole harmony will be incomparably melodious. The Queen's Grace, by her presence, will calm all noise so that your notes will echo across the quiet water and pierce every hearer's heart. Grace a God, young masters, music is a noble art!"

They liked Master Laneham for his love of music. They would do their best, they said, and they set off in haste by a path now well known, for the Park. They had no chance to practice the etiquette of knocking. The music room door was open and Master Goldingham, a big red-faced, black bearded man, was fiercely beating time while Harry Golding sang and the viols played.

They learned much music in those next days. On the last morning they rehearsed inside the dolphin. The music sounded strange and they felt strange too. They had been given pages' costumes, peach-colored doublets and hose with buttons of silver gilt. Oliver's doublet was too big and James's brown cap with the pheasant feather was too tight. However, they were both better off than Harry Golding.

He had been given a mask that was supposed to make his cheerful fat freckled face look like a Greek statue's.

"I'll not wear it," he said and sounded like a sick crow. "I can't breathe in the thing and that's the truth."

Master Goldingham took Harry ashore and walked up and down with him. There were windows in the sides of the dolphin to let air in and music out. Oliver could see Master Goldingham talking and smiling and after a moment Harry laughed and slapped his knee, shouting, "Aye, I'll do it!" but he sang his part without the mask that day.

He had it on the next evening when the dolphin slid along the bridge where the Queen was sitting among her ladies. It was as Master Laneham had said. Her presence had thrown a silence not just over the crowd of nobles on the bridge but on everyone who stood along the lake or perched on the castle walls.

You could almost, Oliver thought, hear the banners moving on the towers and the fountains splashing in the garden. He could hear James draw a long breath and the boy beside him rub rosin on his bow. Then Harry counted softly—one, two, three, four—and began to sing.

He sounded worse than a sick crow!

A voice from the shore shouted, "What's the matter, Arion?"

Harry yelled, "I am none of Arion. I am honest Harry Golding!" and whipped off the mask.

Then everyone around the lake laughed. Oliver could see the Queen laughing harder than anyone. In a moment the silence was mended as suddenly as it had been broken. Harry's voice rose out of it, the viols and the other voices followed in their turn and it was—as Master Laneham said afterwards—incomparably melodious.

The musicians were all at supper in the great hall. Master Laneham called it an ambrosial banquet. There were hundreds of dishes offered to the Queen but she ate little and soon left the hall. Then Oliver saw that what Master Doughty had said was true. In a few moments the splendid game pies, the whole salmon in jelly, the spiced hams and roasted capons were hacked and torn to pieces.

James said over a plate of scraps, "We eat better than this in your mother's kitchen."

Oliver found a chicken bone to gnaw at and said, "But look at Harry's plate. He has enough for Arion and the dolphin too."

Harry Golding's plate was certainly well heaped. He was saying, "Aye, the Queen said it was the best part of the show, but it was none of my doing. It was Master Goldingham thought how to bring me out from under that mask, in which I could sing no more than a cat under a haystack!"

James was not looking at Harry but at someone behind Oliver who said in a silky voice, "And it's here they are, Master Hatton—the two young musicians of whom I told you."

Oliver knew that voice. He knew as he turned that he would see Master Doughty and there he was in white velvet with a scarf of purple laced with silver. He looked as splendid as his master who was Christopher Hatton, captain of the Queen's bodyguard. Of course Master Doughty talked more, and more cleverly than Master Hatton.

During one of Master Doughty's rare flashes of silence Master Hatton spoke about the cittern and about the music from the dolphin. Then someone came up to ask him when the dancing would begin and he smiled and turned away. Master

Doughty started to follow him but paused as Oliver said, "But where is Master Drake?"

Master Doughty shrugged his velvet shoulders. "Why, where would he be then? Rubbing the sides of ships with the ends of tallow candles, tarring ropes, varnishing spars—at Plymouth, lad, at Plymouth! Where else?"

"Will he sail soon?" Oliver asked.

"Why," said Master Doughty, "that's as the Queen pleases and as the wind blows, from Spain one minute, from France the next. Women are weathercocks. Queens and all. Time will tell, lad—time will tell."

Oliver drew his black brows together. His eyes shone very blue between his thick lashes. His face, usually rather pale, flushed slightly.

"You should not speak so of the Queen's Grace," he said in a half-choked voice and then found himself sneezing. By the time his third sneeze was over, Master Doughty had slipped back into the crowd. The Queen came back into the hall and the dancing began.

When they saw Master Doughty again he was dancing a pavane and Oliver had to admit that he was one of the stateliest and most graceful dancers there. Even Master Hatton, the Queen's partner, danced no better. Master Doughty's partner was dressed in white silk embroidered with gold butterflies and pearls. She had a net of gold and pearls over her dark hair. As she turned towards them Oliver heard James give a groan that was almost a growl. Master Doughty's partner was Isabel Desmond.

She nodded to them as she passed by in the dance. Oliver had been proud of his peach-colored suit up to the time Isabel looked at him. Now he felt like a country lout dressed in clothes too big for him. James must have been feeling much the same.

He said, "If I'd ever learned to dance, I'd show him!"

Sir George Desmond was leaning against a marble pillar. He smiled at Isabel as she passed. He looked through James and Oliver as if they had been made of rather dusty window glass.

The music changed. They were dancing a sarabande now and the Earl of Leicester, splendid in white and gold, was the Queen's partner. Master Doughty was still dancing with Isabel. Master Hatton was standing behind Oliver.

He heard someone say to Master Hatton, "Your secretary moves with much grace, Master Hatton, and so does his partner. Who is she?"

The speaker was a plump pink-faced young man stuffed into a handsome suit of blue velvet slashed with silver. Master Hatton told him that the young lady was the daughter of Sir George Desmond of Campions' in Lincolnshire. Sir George was an old friend of Master Doughty's in Ireland, he said. They had come to Kenilworth at Master Doughty's invitation.

"I would like well to dance with her," the young man said.

Master Hatton laughed kindly. "So would others, my lord," he said.

However, when the sarabande was over, he led the young nobleman up to Master Doughty and when the music began again, Isabel had a new partner. Master Doughty strolled over to Sir George who had found a new pillar to lean on.

He talked more than usual, Oliver noticed, and Master Doughty rather less, shrugging his shoulders. Once he looked at him and James and Oliver thought he was talking about them but Sir George never turned his eyes in their direction.

Perhaps I'm mistaken, Oliver thought. Yet he felt sure he was not.

Master Doughty went back to Isabel when the dance ended.

James had never taken his eyes off her. To him all the candles seemed lighted to shine only on her. The great tapestried hall had been built only for her to dance in. The music marked time only for her feet.

He said suddenly, "I've had enough. I'm going. How about you?"

They hardly spoke on the way home.

Once Oliver said, "It's strange that Master Doughty never told us he knew Sir George. And why did he not go to Campions' when he was here—or did he?—at night perhaps while we slept?"

James stumbled over the root of a tree and said crossly, "What's strange about one snake knowing another?"

Oliver laughed and said, "I thought all the snakes were chased out of Ireland long since."

"Yes," said James, "and those two came here. Oh, why did you say no when Isabel offered to teach us to dance?"

James had refused to learn too but Oliver did not remind him of that.

He only said, "I wish we'd learned," and they went the rest of the way in silence.

As they took off their new clothes, James said, "She danced better than anyone, didn't she, Oliver?"

"Except the Queen," Oliver said.

"I never looked at the Queen," said James, "and as for that Thomas Doughty, I hope I never see him again."

They did not see him for nearly two years.

Of those two years Oliver had only a confused memory. It was as if the visit to Kenilworth were a rocket that blazed so brightly that everything beyond it was darkness. He worked in the shop now instead of studying Latin. He hardly ever saw

Isabel Desmond except as a distant figure on a horse, sometimes with Joyce beside her. He practiced on his viol. He swam and fished and crossed Boston Harbor on errands. He would hear there whatever news the latest ship brought in. Most of it was about the Queen and never the same two days running.

On Monday she was going to marry a French prince. On Tuesday she was to marry a Dutchman and rule the Netherlands. On Wednesday there was a new plot against her life, some of King Philip's work. On Thursday she was generous, openhanded and Queen of the sea. On Friday her quarrel with Spain was made up, all shipbuilding stopped and she was the stingiest sovereign England had ever known. On Saturday? Well, no ship came in on Saturday so people talked about Drake's next voyage.

Where was he going? Why, to Morocco, to Brazil, Java, north around America to China, to the Spanish Main! What did it matter so long as it was Drake?

After the evening music was over they would talk about him sometimes round the fire on windy winter nights, but he grew less and less real as the months slipped away. There was his letter saying that they had done their errand well and the Queen, besides sending fair words about the cittern, had praised them for their music. Master Doughty had spoken well of them too, the letter said.

Mistress Barrett had been happy at this news. "I always said Master Doughty would help you at court and he will help Master Drake too, you mark my words," she said.

It was no use telling her that Master Doughty had never even spoken to them until after the Queen had seen them. When they told her that it was not Master Doughty but Master Drake who was known all over England as the man who would teach the King of Spain a lesson, she would simply repeat that they would hear of Master Doughty again and send them to bed.

A year went by and some dark months of another year. Then one morning there were snowdrops in bloom and, almost without Oliver's seeing what came between, roses and it was June again and his fourteenth birthday. His father had made him a new viol da gamba. The next evening he went to Campions' to ask the priest for a lesson on it.

This was a new priest, Father Ambrose, a brown-faced melancholy courteous man, a skilled musician, a great lover of gardens. When Oliver found him he was working among the yews, deftly clipping a spray here and there so that the elephant would still raise his trunk boldly, the ship still sail in the lightest wind.

He admired the viol, said he would be glad to put his poor skill at Oliver's service, added that before he touched anything so handsome he must wash his hands.

"That polish makes the wood shine like a glass of Spanish wine with the sunshine through it, yes?" he said.

He paused a moment to show Oliver the knight in armor.

"See," he said, "a rose is climbing up it. I mean to train it to make the bridle a rein of red roses on each side. You like the idea, I hope. Yes?"

He spoke good English, a little better perhaps than most people born within sight of Boston Stump. He put his r's where they belonged and rolled them slightly, Oliver noticed.

The lesson was a short one because Isabel and her father soon came into the garden. Oliver could not bear to let Isabel hear his first efforts. He put the viol and the bow back into the case. He would have started home but Sir George Desmond showed him unusual hospitality.

"You must take some refreshment after your ride," Sir George said. "Oh—you came in a boat? Why, then, you need food even more. A horse bears the burden when a man rides, but in a boat he pulls his own weight and the boat's weight too. And, speaking of seafaring things, have you heard from Master Drake lately? I saw Master Drake in Ireland not many months ago, and of course his friend Master Thomas Doughty, an old neighbor of ours in Ireland. They were talking of a voyage—now where was it he said they were going—Morocco? Italy? I forget."

This was a great deal of conversation from Sir George. More, in fact, than Oliver had ever heard from him in his life.

He answered truthfully that he had seen Master Drake only once and that was two years ago. He knew nothing about any voyage, he said.

"And would not tell if you did," said fat-fisted Jonas Oak who appeared suddenly at his elbow.

Oak ended his sentence with a short yapping laugh. For a heavily built man Oak had a surprisingly quick way of moving. He had been behind one of the clipped yews, Oliver supposed, where he could listen to what was said. Only what did he expect to hear?

Isabel scowled at Oak but said nothing. She had looked pretty a moment before, but now, in spite of her fine clothes—a green silk dress, a green velvet hat with a whole nest of feathers clasped by emeralds and pearls—she was only a sulky-looking girl. She was not, Oliver noticed, quite so slender as when she had danced the pavane at Kenilworth.

Oak looked sidewise at Oliver out of his little pale gray eyes. He picked a rose, crushed it in one of his thick hands, thrust it against his purplish nose, then scattered the petals on the grass.

"Come," he said. "Enough nonsense. Tell us where he sails—and when."

There was a strange silence in the garden. It reminded Oliver of something. What was it? Something about Father Andrew. He felt as if he were going to be beaten for not knowing his Latin and the first blow had not yet fallen. He felt himself stiffen so he would not cry out at the pain.

Father Ambrose said quietly, "Oliver would wish to share any news he had with his friends, I feel sure, Master Oak."

Sir George Desmond straightened himself up from the statue against which he had been leaning.

"Tell the groom to bring the horses, Oak," he said. "Since you'll take no refreshment, Oliver, you'll excuse us, I hope. We have just time for a ride before the sun goes down."

The priest walked down to the wharf with Oliver.

"I always hoped sometime I would see Master Drake," he said. "One of England's greatest men, brave in danger, patient in the face of misfortune, gentle to the weak. It's natural for us all to wish to know what he is doing for our country in these dangerous days."

Oliver's tongue was soon loosened and he told all he knew about Master Drake. After all, it was not much, little more than all men knew. If Father Ambrose was disappointed, he gave no sign. He listened with interest and when they reached the wharf, asked Oliver to come back soon for another lesson. He never went because Master Drake's letter to Stephen Barrett came. Master Ward, captain of a ship from Plymouth, brought it. They had been delayed first by fog, then by head winds, he said. The letter might have come more quickly by land, he added.

Stephen Barrett read it in silence. Then he handed it to his wife who also read it but not quietly. She exclaimed, "Lord a mercy" or groaned at the end of every sentence, smiled, shook her head, wiped her eyes with her handkerchief.

At last she sighed, "I always said Master Doughty would help them. Well, my lads, you must pack your cloak-bags again, I suppose!"

"You are willing they should go then?" Stephen Barrett asked.

"Where?" the boys gasped. "When?"

"Why, on a voyage with Master Doughty to Morocco or wherever the Queen bids Frank Drake go, as two of his musicians, Master Doughty having said how well you did your parts at Kenilworth. You must take your viol da gamba as well as your viol da braccia, Oliver. And take your cittern too and teach James one or the other since his voice may change any time now... Nonsense, James, of course you can learn to play the viol. Well, a trumpet then... Give him a trumpet, Stephen... What, no trumpets? Well, a drum then, give him a drum..."

"You are to sail back to Plymouth with Captain Ward. I must see your shirts are well washed." She bustled off calling, "Polly... Nancy, Bess... soap... hot water," leaving the boys and Stephen Barrett staring silently at each other.

There were three busy days before the ship sailed. Everyone worked to get them ready. Even Joyce helped let out seams to make their peach-colored doublets big enough.

One bright morning when the shadows of the yews were still dark on the dewy grass, they went to hear Mass at Campions' and to say good-bye to Isabel.

"Oliver is going to Morocco," Joyce told Isabel, "and he's going to bring me back a gold colored horse with a silver mane."

"And with emerald eyes, I suppose," James said.

"No," Joyce said seriously, "eyes like brown velvet, like Isabel's."

"We'll bring you each one," James promised and Isabel smiled and said, "Then come back soon."

The wind blew them quickly to Plymouth. It was not long before they left the Eddystone roaring behind them. Dawn was coming up when Captain Ward said to Oliver, "There's Plymouth Hoe!"

Stephen Barrett had always said, "The grass is a little greener there than anywhere else in the world."

Perhaps, Oliver used to think, that was only to eyes that had seen nothing but sea and sky for weeks. It couldn't, he thought, be greener than the lawns at Campions' in June. Yet even after his first few days at sea, even in November, the bowling green on the Hoe looked as green as Isabel's silk dress—or greener.

There were gardens near the Hoe and in one of them Master Drake was walking up and down. The man with him was John Brewer, a trumpeter of Master Hatton's, Oliver learned later. He had evidently said something Master Drake did not like. His eyes flashed blue fire, his face was red above his red-gold beard.

"I will hear no tales against Master Doughty," he said angrily in his trumpet voice. "This has been told me thrice at least— that Master Doughty has told Lord Burghley of our voyage though the Queen commanded that he should know nothing of it. Some add that he has sold the secret to the King of Spain and will betray me when we are at sea and what else, I know not. But this I do know. Master Doughty is my friend. He has risked all he had—a thousand crowns—to make this voyage with me. Why would he choose the dangers I face when he might live softly at court, dance the pavane with the Queen, read Latin in rose gardens, eat venison pasty? Why does he choose to eat salt beef in a gale and die of scurvy mayhap?

Why? For friendship, Master Brewer, and such a friend I wish all true men. Does he hope to put gold in his pockets? Why, so do we all—even the Queen's Grace. And when this voyage is made, I promise you the meanest boy in the crew will be a gentleman."

He had not seemed to see Oliver and James, but those widely opened blue eyes of his missed little.

"And these young masters have come just in time to make music on more than one ocean and they'll have something to bring home for their trouble, I warrant. The sea will test them, the sea will test us all, Master Brewer. It has a way of bringing out the truth."

Brewer said, "I hope these pages of yours can keep secrets, sir."

"You mean I talk too much," Drake said smiling. "But it is hardly a secret that my Lord Burghley would keep peace with the King of Spain at any price and that I would strike a blow for our Queen where it will hurt him most. Have I told you or anyone where I think that place is or whether we sail east or west to reach it? Besides, Master Brewer, we sail today. If my pages know secrets, to whom will they tell them—gulls? dolphins? flying fish?"

Master Brewer did not answer these questions. Two other men and a boy were coming into the garden.

Master Drake said to the boy, "John, these are the musicians of whom I spoke, Oliver Barrett and James Campion. Help them get aboard the *Pelican*. This is my kinsman, John Drake," he added.

Oliver had guessed it already from John's likeness to Master Drake. Like him, John Drake was strongly built. He had the same widely spaced eyes though his were greenish hazel rather than blue. From the first, in bad days or in good ones, he was their friend.

He showed them the five ships of Master Drake's fleet and told them their names and the names of their captains. The largest, of which Drake himself was the captain, was the *Pelican*, one hundred tons. Then came the *Elizabeth*, eighty tons—Captain John Winter. Much smaller was the bark *Marigold*, thirty tons—Captain John Thomas. The *Swan*, a flyboat, was fifteen tons. Her captain was John Chester. There was also a pinnace of fifteen tons, the *Benedict*.

"Thomas Moone is her captain," John Drake said. "See, there he is on deck."

"Not Thomas Moone who was at Nombre de Dios!" Oliver said.

"None other," said John.

To see Thomas Moone made what had seemed like a dream begin to come true. There he was, as sturdy as a ship built with his own hands, a big, bearded, blue-eyed man, a man who had helped take Nombre de Dios, who had set up pinnaces in secret harbors, who had made Stephen Barrett's crutches! The boys had listened many times to Stephen Barrett's stories of that great expedition, from which Drake's ships had returned ballasted with gold and silver. Now Thomas Moore was here with them, and they felt the voyage could begin.

CHAPTER 6

GENTLEMAN ADVENTURER

THE VOYAGE began on the afternoon of the fifteenth of November, 1577, at five o'clock. From the first it went badly. A violent storm came up that night. The *Pelican* was dismasted and the *Marigold* damaged. The whole fleet had to put back into Plymouth. It was four weeks before they could sail again.

When Oliver looked back on the voyage his memories of sailing the Atlantic were not of great tempests, of islands rising out of the sea, of flying fish or tropical calms, but of Thomas Doughty. From the first the troubles of the voyage revolved around him. For a long time Drake could not—or would not—see that the man to whom he had always shown friendship was really his enemy.

Before they crossed the Atlantic they added an important prize, the *Mary*, to the fleet. As a mark of confidence Drake put Thomas Doughty in command of this ship. By this time everyone in the fleet had learned that they were not on a trading voyage to Morocco. They were to sail through the Straits of Magellan and attack the King of Spain's ships in the Pacific.

Almost at once there began to be mutinous talk, loudest wherever Thomas Doughty was.

Men who listened to him began to say openly that it was foolhardy to try to make the desperate passage of the Straits of Magellan. Why freeze and drown when they might easily sail to the West Indies and capture treasure ships there? That would hurt King Philip just as much as anything that could be done in the Pacific, Oliver heard the sailors say. It was easy enough for Thomas Doughty to stir up fears about the Straits. Many ships had been lost there since Magellan's voyage and the sailors knew it.

Round Drake's table in the *Pelican's* cabin everything still seemed as harmonious as the music of the viols. Before they played and sang, Oliver and James served the food on silver plates with gilded borders and the Drake arms in the center. Even the pans in which they brought the food from the galley were of pure silver. There were fine damask napkins and bowls of scented water for use between courses, silver spoons with gilded bowls, silver cups and a great salt cellar with the Drake arms on it.

John Brewer blew his trumpet when the meal was ready. The gentlemen adventurers came to the table. Master Doughty always sat next to Drake and Drake served him from his own dish. After the food was served, the music of the viols began. Sometimes James sang. Sometimes John Drake danced a morris dance. Oliver would play the tune for the dance on a recorder and the bells bound below John's knees would ring loud as he leaped to the roof of the cabin.

There were prayers on deck after dinner and sermons on Sundays and sometimes on other days if the chaplain thought they were needed. The chaplain was Master Francis Fletcher,

a great admirer of Master Doughty. Master Fletcher told Oliver that Master Doughty's gifts were rare, that he was a most sweet orator, a philosopher and knew Latin, Greek and Hebrew. All this was true, no doubt, but Oliver felt that in a storm at sea or in a fight with a Spanish ship, Master Drake, who knew no Latin, even, would get more help from some tarry-fisted mariner than he would from Thomas Doughty. Drake himself never hesitated to lend a hand at the ropes in times of danger, but the gentlemen adventurers had been taught by Master Doughty that they were too good for such work.

One of the adventurers was Thomas Doughty's brother, John. He too was in favor of gentlemen behaving like gentlemen and of a voyage to the West Indies rather than to the Pacific. The sailors feared both brothers and for a strange reason: they were sure that both Doughtys were magicians and could make the wind blow as they pleased.

Oliver heard something muttered by one of the sailors about Thomas Doughty's cap case. When Oliver asked him what he meant by that, the man said that Thomas Doughty was a conjurer and kept the winds shut up in the case in which he kept his cap. If he opened it only a little, there would be a breeze, not this flat calm in which they were all broiling. He could make it blow fresh and brisk and send them all to death in those accursed Straits for which they were bound.

Oliver could see that the man was really afraid.

"Master Drake must know these things," Oliver said to James. "Why does he bear it?" But James had no answer.

The sea was so calm that they had both been swimming near the *Pelican*. Now they were on deck, drying themselves.

Oliver added, "Perhaps he feels that by patience and kindness he can win Master Doughty to think as he does, and that then all will go well with the voyage."

"Do you think he believes that Thomas Doughty keeps the winds in his cap case?" James asked.

Oliver did not answer at once. A flying fish leaped on the deck of the ship. Its wings began to dry in the hot still air. Soon they would be brittle and useless and it would die. Oliver threw it back into the sea and watched it as it took another flying leap. Flying fish leaped, he knew, because they were being chased by fierce hungry fish much larger than themselves.

"I think," he said at last, "that our Captain half believes it. He is surrounded by dangers and must choose which is worse and leap from one to another, yet never look at the danger. Perhaps Master Drake would rather believe the winds are in Thomas Doughty's cap case than see that his best friend is a traitor to him."

"He may be patient too long," James said.

Drake's patience had seemed endless but at last it broke.

Thomas Doughty was accused of stealing things from the *Mary's* cargo. Drake swore he did not believe it, but when he investigated, he found that Doughty had some things belonging to the passengers in his possession. Doughty said that they were presents and accused Thomas Drake, Master Drake's youngest brother, of accepting presents too.

It was then that Drake's patience was exhausted.

"I doubt not it is Francis rather than Thomas you mean to disparage," he said furiously, "and by God's life I will not suffer it." He ordered Doughty back to the *Pelican* and put Thomas Drake in command of the *Mary*. One of the gentlemen adventurers prayed Drake to forgive Doughty. Drake said that he did and he seemed to forget all that had passed, but he stayed on board the *Mary*.

Their goal was the coast of Brazil but it came no nearer. They were still becalmed on a Sunday when John Brewer came across from the *Pelican* to report more trouble. Someone was trying to stir the crew to mutiny and sail the *Pelican* away to the Spanish Main.

"What do you know about this, Francis Fletcher?" Drake asked the chaplain.

Fletcher usually stayed on board the *Pelican* but he had been brought over to the *Mary* for the Sunday service. As was usual on Sunday, everyone was dressed in his best and the rigging of the ship was hung with flags and banners. They dropped limply against the sails with no wind to set them flying.

Chaplain Fletcher said that he had heard some talk of mutiny on the *Pelican*. It was true that men were saying that it would be an easy matter to seize her, as soon as the wind rose, slip away from the fleet and sail for the Spanish Main. He thought it was only idle talk for idle days, the sort of thing sailors say when the ship is becalmed. He had spoken to Master Doughty about it. He had thought the same.

"Why did you not report to me?" Master Drake asked quietly.

"As I say, because to me it seemed only vain and idle murmurings. Moreover when I spoke to Master Doughty about it, he asked me to say nothing since he would be accused of stirring up the trouble."

Master Drake said, still speaking quietly, "Tell me about this talk so I can judge how idle it was."

John Brewer told how Cuttill, master of the *Pelican*, had been told by Master Doughty that if Cuttill would steer for the Spanish Main and go on the account—the courteous way of saying become a pirate—when they got back to London with their pockets well lined, Cuttill would have no trouble with the Admiralty.

"I'll keep you safe in the Temple," Master Doughty had said to Cuttill, "and no officer from the Admiralty, not the Lord High Admiral himself, shall get you."

"He did but jest," the chaplain put in hastily.

Drake's reply was to order a boat overside to bring Master Doughty to him.

The *Pelican* was becalmed some distance off. Master Fletcher was preaching one of his long sermons when the boat came back with Thomas Doughty in it.

Master Drake walked to the rail and looked down at him. For a moment neither spoke. Then Doughty stood up and put his hands against the ship, offering to come aboard.

Drake's voice rang out: "Stay where you are, Thomas Doughty, for I must send you to another place," he said.

He commanded the mariners to take Master Doughty to the *Swan*, saying, "It is a place more fit for you than the one from which you came."

Master Doughty begged to come aboard and speak with Drake but Drake refused to listen. So, in utter disgrace, Doughty went to the *Swan* as a prisoner. She was the smallest of the fleet. Her crew was small. She carried stores, food, spare sails and rope. John Chester was her captain, John Sarocold her master. They were men Drake trusted. Probably he felt that Thomas Doughty could do little harm there. Yet at the last moment he called Oliver to him.

"This is not an order, Oliver," he said quietly, "but I need your help. Will you go to the *Swan* too? Help Sarocold keep order there? Report to me what takes place? I trust you to judge fairly, to speak with honesty. These are hard days," he added. "Sometimes I do not know how to go through them. If your father were here—"

"I'll go, of course, sir," Oliver said.

So Oliver went to the *Swan.*

Doughty's disgrace had not silenced his tongue. He was lying on a bunk in the cabin, talking to Captain Chester, when Oliver came in. He was not in irons. He was lying with his hands back of his neck and his long elegant feet higher than his head.

"Ah!" he said, seeing Oliver, "so we are to have music as well as an extra spy. How generous of our much loved general! Take pen and paper, Master Spy, and write: 'I found T. Doughty lying with his feet in the air, trying to corrupt the Captain of the *Swan* (fifteen tons) and get him to attack the Spanish treasure fleet...' Now here's my plan— take note of all I say. Why sail south with difficulty when we can fly north with ease? With a little luck, a little courage, we can take a fregata of—say—twenty tons. Next one of forty, and so on. Before you know it, we'll have the whole Spanish fleet at our mercy. Let them carry the treasure across the Isthmus for us and load the ships at Nombre de Dios for us. We'll take the ships, man, and sail them home loaded with gold and emeralds and by home I mean not England but the Emerald Isle. And we'll hang our treasure round the necks of the prettiest girls in the world, half Irish, half Spanish—or don't you agree with me, Master Spy? Ah well, we have carrot-haired ones too. Red or black, we suit all tastes."

Oliver felt himself flushing.

Captain Chester said laughing, "Oh, Tom, you will have your jest no matter where or when!" but Oliver thought, Only he is not quite jesting.

Doughty talked in the same way at meals. He had ordered a south wind—to please their spies, he said. The wind now blew

from the south in bitter icy blasts. John Sarocold, the master, who was trying to sail south against it, was so angry that he refused to eat at the Captain's table but messed forward with the crew.

Soon Doughty accused Sarocold of giving the sailors better food than the adventurers had. He said to the Captain, "I marvel, Master Chester, that you take it at Sarocold's hands to be so ill used," and added to Sarocold, "You and your mates eat plentifully while we are on the point to starve. Even your fellow spy is starving."

Sarocold said, "Such rascals as you should be glad to eat the leather off the oars."

The food on the *Swan* was poor enough, Oliver thought, but no one was starving. Even he had enough to eat, though he spent his time on decks hauling on ropes at Sarocold's orders while Doughty lay on his bunk reading the Iliad.

"Master Chester," he said. "Let us not be so used at these knaves' hands. Lose nothing of the authority Drake gave you. Take the sword into your own hands. As to these rascals, let them cut each other's throats. You know well," he said with one of his twisting smiles, "that Drake owes his command to me and that we were sent on the voyage with equal authority."

Oliver said quietly, "Master Drake owes his command to the Queen."

Doughty laughed and Sarocold ground his teeth in anger and said, "If there are enemies and traitors to General Drake on this voyage, he would do well to deal with them as Magellan did, which was to hang them up as an example to the rest."

Doughty only shrugged his shoulders, and said, "Nay, softly, his authority is none such as Magellan's was. As for hanging, it is for dogs, not men."

Then he turned his back on Sarocold and said to Oliver, "But why is the cittern silent after we have consumed these delicate feasts? Come! A tune, Master Spy! Play us 'Once there was a Spanish lady and she loved an Englishman.'"

"I don't know it," Oliver said.

"No—nor ever will, neither you nor your sandy-haired cousin, I'll be bound. Well, play us a pavane. Surely you know a pavane."

Oliver had an impulse to break the cittern over Master Doughty's head. Sarocold saved both head and cittern by saying, "On the deck, if you will, Master Barrett. Your fingers are needed for something more important than strumming."

They had been separated from the rest of the fleet for many weeks but at last they met the *Pelican*. Drake had sailed far south along the coast of Brazil and then north again looking for the *Swan*. He decided to reduce the number of his ships so it would be easier to keep the fleet together. The *Swan* was brought alongside the *Pelican* in a sheltered bay. Her cargo was transferred to Drake's ship. They saved the *Swan's* ironwork and broke her up for firewood.

Oliver was glad enough to see the last of her. He was with Drake when Sarocold made his report of the things Doughty had said.

"You heard this too, Oliver?" Drake asked him.

"Yes, it is true," Oliver said. "The words are as Master Sarocold has repeated them. But I am not sure that Master Doughty always means what he says. It's as if his tongue speaks more than he means to say, more than he believes, even. He called me a spy a dozen times a day. Yet I doubt if he believed it, only when he has talked enough he believes what he has said—and others believe him too."

What Drake believed, he did not say.

By June they had reached the coast of Patagonia.

CHAPTER 7

LAND OF THE GIANTS

OLIVER WAS with Chaplain Fletcher on a sandy piece of shore

when he heard the chaplain exclaim loudly, "Giants!"

Oliver looked around. Except for members of their own crew getting wood and water, there was no one in sight. Then he saw, close to one of Fletcher's rather small feet, an enormous bare footprint and others like it along the beach.

That was all they saw of the giants that day but it was enough to frighten the sailors. Fletcher was sure that the Patagonians were not only giants but conjurers. Every time the wind whirled sand into the air or covered the coast with fog he said that the giants were weaving spells. Once Drake went ashore and vanished in one of these fogs but was rescued by John Chester.

Another day Oliver and James with some others from the *Pelican's* crew were on an island close to the mainland where at low tide men could cross on foot. They heard loud shouts from the mainland and there were the giants, leaping, dancing, holding up their hands and crying out. They stopped on a hill half a mile from the water side and two of them came running down to the water with great speed and grace.

Drake sent them knives and bells and bugles—such things as he thought would please them—but they would not come near enough to take them. Oliver tied the things to a rod and stuck it up in the sand. Then he crossed back to the island and watched while the giants took the things. They left a bundle of ostrich feathers in payment and went off to their friends, leaping and dancing.

James said, "They are not really giants. I saw none over seven and a half feet. Why, there are Englishmen almost as tall in the fleet."

"Yes," Oliver said, "and the porter at the gate at Kenilworth and the trumpeters were taller."

Drake stayed near the island some time having the ships cleaned and letting his men rest after the long voyage. After the first day the Patagonians became less afraid of the visitors. They brought legs of ostriches, which the English cooked and found to taste rather like roast mutton. They might not be giants to Oliver but they towered above Drake. Once one of them standing beside him reached down and snatched from Drake's head a scarlet sea cap that he wore. Then, as if thinking Drake might be angry, he took an arrow and wounded himself deeply in the leg.

"What does he mean by that?" one of the sailors growled.

"Why, that he loves me dearly and would shed his blood for me so that his friend ought not to be angry about a small thing like a cap," Drake said.

He always, Oliver noticed, seemed to have a natural under-standing of savage people. It was based on kindness and in most cases it was returned. Drake liked to see the naked Patagonian babies being basted near the fire with ostrich oil and chalk. This mixture dried on their skin and kept them warm in those bitter winds. He liked the way the men rolled up their long hair and used it like a bag to carry things in—toothpicks, arrows, fire sticks. He enjoyed watching them make fire, spinning a hard round piece of wood like holly on a flat soft one like fir and dropping pieces of dry rushes into it when it glowed.

He was especially interested in their musical instruments which were boxes of bark, sewn with ostrich gut like lute strings. They put little stones in them which rattled when they danced. They hung them at their belts and the higher they leaped the louder the noise; the louder the noise the more they danced.

They would die dancing, Oliver thought, if some friend did not snatch away the rattle. Then they would stand for a long time not knowing where they were.

One day Drake sent his musicians ashore to play for them. They liked the music of viols, but the sound of trumpets was terrible to them. Oliver always remembered playing that day. It was a bright clear day, almost windless. Smoke from fires made to honor Setebos, the Patagonians' god, rose straight into the air. The musicians sat on some rocks on one side of the beach and the giants on the sand at the other side. They were freshly painted with black and yellow and white paint. Some had one shoulder painted black and the other white, with white moons on the black and black suns on the white. The women were dressed in their best with furs round their shoulders or waists. While the viols played they were quite happily chewing raw seal meat or ostrich legs, basting their babies with ostrich oil, waving bunches of ostrich plumes. When the music was over they threw down their bunches of feathers in front of the players and asked for nothing in return. However, Drake sent them some small bells and they danced off with a great chiming over the hill.

The giants had no boats and they were afraid of the sea. If their children wandered close to the water, they snatched them away, moaning and roaring. On one side of the bay a great whaleback of rock ran into the icy water. It was connected with the land by a bar of sand and pebbles by which it could be reached at low tide, but it was an island most of the day and at high tide it was completely covered.

One day a small Patagonian boy, bolder than his giant father and uncles, crossed to the whaleback at low tide and sat playing in the little seaweed-lined pool on the whale's head. When his mother saw him, the tide had already covered the bar but the water was no more than a foot deep. The woman was more than six feet tall and could easily have waded out but she only stood there roaring out the child's name. Oliver was playing his viol in the *Pelican's* cabin and did not hear her at first, but when the music was over, he heard the noise and came out on deck to see what caused it.

Chaplain Fletcher, always interested in the customs of strange people, was trying to write down what the woman was saying.

"It sounds," he said to Oliver, "like Maquinchanyagogtoo. Strange, is it not, that mother-love propels not the woman through the water in search of her young? Why even the civet cat, even the tigress—"

"Stranger still to sit writing and preaching about it and let him drown," Oliver said.

"Surely there's plenty of time. We can send a boat," the chaplain said.

"The crew have taken all the boats to go fishing," Oliver said.

The mother's voice had summoned many of her tribe. They all stood there moaning and wailing. A little wind made the water splash and foam as it rose around the whale back.

"What do you suggest I do?" the chaplain asked peevishly, shutting his notebook.

"Why, nothing," Oliver said. He had already stripped off his jerkin and shirt.

He heard the mother's desperate wail.

"Maquin chan ya gog too—" Yes, that was what she said. And now the child had heard her and was crying too and stumbling towards her.

"I'm coming, Mack," Oliver called and dived into the harbor.

The icy water was like the cold stings of ten thousand bees. It almost stopped his breathing. At first he could hardly move. Then he began to cut through the gray waves. The rock had looked close to the ship but it slid away from him as he swam, and the voices of the giants grew no louder. Then suddenly the whaleback loomed dark above him. He found a foothold slippery with weed, a weed-covered projection, slippery too under his blue fingers, and hauled himself out of the water.

His teeth chattered as he said, "Here I am, Mack, up you go. Legs round my neck, arms round my head. Let's take a ride."

The boy seemed to understand. He began to laugh.

"He jounced as if he were riding an ostrich," Oliver told James later.

Mack, as Oliver called him from then on, was by no means ready to stop his ride when Oliver waded across the sand bar. He gave a fine Patagonian roar when Oliver tried to detach him and hand him to his mother. It was even harder to escape from oily giant hugs and stinging slaps on the back. Oliver found himself shivering in the center of a circle of shouting giants. Pebbles rattled in his ears. An ostrich leg only partly gnawed was thrust into his hand. Bunches of feathers were tossed at his feet. The women gathered driftwood and made a fire to warm him. He found himself chewing seal blubber and liking it. He was rubbed with ostrich oil. Furs were thrown around him. Everyone danced around him. Oliver danced too.

When at last one of the *Pelican's* boats came for him the wails of grief were as loud as they had been for Maquinchany-agogtoo. The next time he went ashore his friends seized him and took him on an ostrich hunt. This was as great an honor as if the Queen had invited him to ride with her at Kenilworth hunting roebucks.

With Master Drake's permission he joined the hunt. These great birds were so strong and swift that it needed much skill to catch them. They were the giants' chief source of food as

well as of oil and feathers so that a hunt was prepared for with great care. They first chose a narrow passage between two hills and fastened nets between trees there. The women and dogs as well as most of the hunters lay hidden there with arrows, stones and clubs.

Oliver had seen the great flocks of ostriches moving through the country and had noticed what the leader of a flock would do to keep his troop in order. If one of his followers moved out of line to the right the leader would move to the left until the wanderer, finding himself alone, would run after the others, flapping his stub wings so fast that he almost rose off the ground.

He had seen how the giants took advantage of this habit to drive the ostriches where they could be trapped, so he knew what to do. The giants gave him an ostrich skin, feathers and all, to put over his head and shoulders. One of the giants dressed in the same way. They both hid in the long grass until a com-

pany of ostriches came along. Then they stooped, pretending to graze, and when the troop had passed they hurried after the flock. Their way of guiding it towards the gap in the hills was this: if they wanted to turn the flock towards the right, they would straggle away towards the left. Then the ostrich leader would move to the right and they would hurry back after him into line. This they did, moving right or left as was needed until the birds were close to the ambush where the nets were set.

Then the giant threw off his ostrich skin, roaring loud. Oliver did the same. The ostriches were frightened and ran forwards into the nets where they were killed by the hidden hunters. The giants gave Oliver bundles of plumes for his day's work. Oliver shared them with James. Both had plans for what they meant to do with the feathers, but at the time neither spoke of them to the other.

Soon after this they sailed south to Port Julian. This was the place where Magellan had hanged two of his men for mutiny. Part of the gallows was still standing. Oliver explored the place and found, below the gallows, bones and a man's skull staring at him. He turned away, shivering in the cold wind that blew always from the south.

Oliver knew that on the *Pelican*, as well as on the *Swan*, Doughty had bragged that he had the power of life and death as Drake had. Drake knew it too, yet he had received Sarocold's report of Doughty's insolence with no sign of anger. Only, Oliver noticed, he looked often towards the spot where Magellan's gallows still stood and at its shadow, long in the early June twilight.

He continued to be patient. Perhaps he still hoped that Thomas Doughty could be won over by kindness. Doughty was under guard on the *Pelican* but not chained or bound or confined to his cabin. Perhaps he mistook Drake's patience for cowardice. At last one day he went too far.

In the hearing of all the crew he made a speech to Drake in which he said that Drake ought to stay in the Atlantic instead of vainly trying to make new discoveries in the Pacific. He said loudly that Drake was risking the lives of everyone in the fleet by trying to pass the Straits of Magellan in such bad weather.

Drake heard him out, then ordered him put in irons and sent to the *Christopher*. Since the *Swan* had been burned, Sarocold had been her master. For the first time since he had known him, Oliver thought that Doughty looked afraid.

"There are desperate and unhonest persons who seek my life there," he stammered.

Drake's answer was to have a tackle rigged and to have Doughty and his brother slung on board the *Christopher*. They were sailing south at the time. A violent storm followed. The *Christopher* vanished in it but was found again in a small bay to the south. Drake decided to treat her as he had the Swan. He first sent the prisoners to Captain Wynter's ship, the *Elizabeth*. He went aboard the ship himself, called all the company together and spoke to them. "I am going to send hither," Oliver heard him say, "a couple of very bad men, which I do not know how to carry along with us on the voyage and go through with it. One is Thomas Doughty, a seditious fellow, and his brother John Doughty, a witch and poisoner. None must speak with them. Take care that they neither set pen to paper nor read but what every man may understand and see."

Did Drake really believe that the Doughtys could cast spells by reading out of books of black magic? Oliver never knew but certainly the sailors believed it.

They broke up the *Christopher* for firewood and sailed south in the long stormy June nights. Since the *Mary* and Thomas Drake were still missing, the fleet was of only three vessels now. They searched for her all along the coast of Patagonia but found no trace of her. Drake would not enter the Straits without her.

He said to Oliver, "The *Mary* will be too short of provisions to make the voyage back to England or to try the Straits alone. I will not enter them until I have sailed north once more."

At last to his great joy he found her not far from Port St Julian. She was covered with weed, leaking badly, and her food was running low.

It was on the *Elizabeth* as it was on every ship Thomas Doughty had ever sailed on. He still tried to stir up men's feelings against the voyage through the Straits. They were almost ready to leave Port St Julian and enter the Straits when Drake at last decided that the presence of Doughty, a man more admired, more trusted by Drake than any friend he had ever had, made the success of the enterprise impossible. Even in Plymouth before they sailed and ever since, men had marveled at Drake's patience at Doughty's arrogance. At last his patience had come to an end. He called together his captains, masters, gentlemen adventurers and the other chief men of the fleet to decide Doughty's fate.

They met on an island opposite the spot on the mainland where the spruce mast, part of Magellan's gallows, still stood with the bones of the men he had executed for mutiny still lying under it.

Oliver could see the mast from where he stood behind his master. This cold June day, one of the shortest of the year, was bright and sunny. Everything he looked at—the mast, the towering rocks across the bay, the wind-bent trees where the giants lay hiding—looked dark against the brightness. The only things that caught the sunlight were the ripples on the blue-green water and ornaments on the clothes of the group of Englishmen. It shone on twisted laces of gold, on slashings of cherry- or emerald-colored silk, on starched ruffs, jewels, velvet caps, feathers.

They were all dressed in their best, as they were on Sundays. Master Drake wore fine dark blue cloth. Thomas Doughty had on black velvet and his cloak with the carnation lining which Oliver remembered ever since the day he had first heard Master Doughty's voice on the muddy shore near Boston. Perhaps the strangest thing about Thomas Doughty that day was that his voice was silent.

As well as the witnesses, there was a jury of forty men gathered to hear and speak in the case against him. The penalty for mutiny is death. All there knew it was so, even if Magellan's gallows had not been there to remind them of it. They knelt on the sand while Master Fletcher prayed for a long time, asking for wisdom to guide them.

After the prayer was over, the trumpets sounded. Oliver could see the giants among the trees leap at the sound. Then Drake stood up and spoke. He said that Thomas Doughty was respected by great men in England, that he himself had felt and still felt for him more than brotherly affection. Yet he had heard many times that Doughty planned the destruction of their voyage. He had been told of this not only at sea but at Plymouth, not only in bare words but in writing, and he had seen it himself in actions tending to overthrow the Queen's service.

He asked for testimony. The witnesses gave it, telling how Master Doughty had boasted that he had equal power of life and death with Drake, how on different ships at different times he had tried to persuade the crews not to enter the Straits but to seize the ship and go on the account, how even before they left Plymouth he had said that they would not risk the passage through the Straits but would sail the Spanish Main and take prizes there. More than one witness said that Burghley, the Lord Treasurer, knew all about the voyage although the Queen said he must not be told since Burghley wanted peace at any price between England and Spain.

Strangely, when he heard this, Doughty burst out, "My Lord Treasurer knew all. He had a plan of the voyage."

"What is that you say?" Drake exclaimed, startled, and there were murmurs of "No, no! Not the Lord Treasurer!" and Oliver heard James mutter, "Why not tell the King of Spain?"

"I gave it to him myself," Thomas Doughty flashed out suddenly, and then was as suddenly silent as if he hardly knew what he had said.

After that there was little doubt of his guilt. He was led away by his guards. The forty men who had been summoned to judge him were left in the last sunlight of the short day to reach their verdict. Before dark they agreed on it.

It was: "Thomas Doughty has deserved death. It stands by no means with our safety to let him live. We remit the manner of his death into the hands of our general, Francis Drake."

Doughty was brought back.

Drake said to the company, "Before we left England, Her majesty the Queen committed her sword to my hands with these words: 'We do account that he which striketh at thee, Drake, striketh at us!' These things you have heard here this day have been against the Queen's Grace."

Then he read the verdict aloud to Doughty, who accepted it quietly. He made two requests—that he might receive Holy

Communion before his death, that he might not die other than a gentleman's death.

According to his request Communion was celebrated two mornings later on the deck of the *Pelican* by Master Fletcher. Drake himself took Communion kneeling beside Doughty. After this they dined. Oliver and James served them. As always, Doughty sat at Drake's right hand, was served from the same silver dish, ate from one of the silver-gilt plates with the Drake arms in the center. They ate cheerfully and quietly together, and took their leave by drinking to each other as if it were only some short journey that was at hand.

After dinner, while the man who was to act as executioner was on shore, making all things ready, Thomas Doughty asked to speak to his friend out of hearing but not out of sight of the others. They stood by the rail of the *Pelican*, talking calmly and quietly. No one has ever known what they said. Then they went ashore and within sight of Magellan's gallows Thomas

Doughty knelt down, took off his ruff and cloak and without dallying or delay prepared his neck for the axe.

He said, smiling at the headsman, "I hope you will not find my neck too short." He asked the others to pray for him and then told the man to do his duty without fear.

Francis Fletcher wrote in his journal of the voyage:

> The worthy manner of his death has blotted out his fault. He was an example of a worthy gentleman who, in seeking for advancement not fit for him, cast himself away. On the island, as our men dug his grave, they found a great grinding stone broken in halves—Magellan's as we suppose. We set one part at his head, the other at his feet, building up the middle with stones and turf. We had cut on the stones his names and the general's name in Latin and the time of his death that those who came after might understand it.

Yet who—thought Oliver—can understand it?

CHAPTER 8

CACAFUEGO

GALES BLEW too furiously to make it possible to enter the Straits.

They spent the rest of the winter on that unhappy island.

Drake, Oliver thought, was never quite the same after Master Doughty's death. He was stern and silent. Lines deepened round his blue eyes and between his eyebrows. He seemed happiest when he was listening to music. James's voice had changed months before. For a long time his notes were hoarse squeaks but he could sing again now in a deeper, stronger voice, so the old tunes sounded in the cabin on cold nights when the wind dashed icy spray against the windows.

Ill feeling between the sailors and the gentlemen adventurers had not stopped with Doughty's execution. It seemed only deepened by cold and misery. At last Drake could bear it no longer. He ordered every man in the fleet to confess his sins and receive Holy Communion. Then—it was the eleventh of August—he ordered the whole company ashore. An open tent was set up for him. He stood in the entrance to it with Captain Thomas of the *Marigold* on one side of him and Captain Wynter of the *Elizabeth* on the other.

Drake began by unfolding a great book of papers he was carrying.

"Shall I now preach a sermon?" Master Fletcher asked, moving importantly towards the tent.

"Nay, soft, Master Fletcher! I must preach this day myself," Drake said.

With that he ordered the men marshaled by ship's companies. When their ranks were in order, he began to speak.

"My masters," he said, "I am a very bad orator, for my bringing up has not been in learning. But what I shall here speak let every man take good notice and let him write it down, for I will speak nothing but answer it in England, yes, and before Her Majesty and I have it here already set down."

Then he opened the book and read what he had written, reminding them of the desperate nature of the voyage, and told them that the mutinies and discords must cease.

"It has even taken my wits from me to think of it," he said. "But, my masters, I must have it left. I must have the gentleman to haul and draw with the mariner and the mariner with the gentleman. What! Let us show ourselves all to be of a company and let us not give occasion to the enemy to rejoice at our decay and overthrow."

Then he offered the *Marigold* to any who feared the prospect of the voyage and who wished to go home.

"But," he said, "let them take heed that they go homeward; for if I find them in my way, I will surely sink them. I must needs be plain with you. I have taken that in hand that I know not how to go through with. It passes my capacity. It bereaves me of my wits to think of it."

He paused. Not a voice was raised for going home. Then he asked their willing obedience. Every man agreed to follow him and to leave his wages to Drake's generosity.

When he had finished speaking to the crews, he startled the officers by discharging each one from his post. Wynter and Thomas protested, asking the reason.

Drake asked sharply, "Is there any reason why I cannot?"

They had no answer but hung their heads.

Drake spoke of Doughty's execution. He deserved death, he said, for his mutinous acts and because, against the Queen's command, he had betrayed the secret of the voyage to Burghley.

"More there are who deserve no other fate," Drake said, "but there shall no more die."

He spoke their names and they humbled themselves on their knees before him.

Then he told the story of how the whole enterprise began. He showed letters and documents including a bill of the Queen's share in the expedition.

"And now, my masters, if this voyage should not have good success, we should be a scorning, a reproachful blot to our whole country forever, and what a triumph it would be to Spain! And again the like would never be attempted."

As Drake paused, it seemed to Oliver that England and Spain hung for a moment in the balance. Then he heard Drake's voice again, with that tone like a trumpet call, saying that he restored each officer to his place.

"And if it be that I never come home," he ended more quietly, "yet will Her Majesty pay every man his wages. It is she indeed whom we all come to serve. And for you to say that you come to serve me, I will not give you thanks, for it is only Her Majesty you serve. The voyage is only of her setting forth."

Then he wished for good fortune and friendship for them all and sent them about their business.

On the seventeenth of August, 1578, they left St Julian's Bay and in three days came to the opening of the dreaded Straits. There were only three ships now. They had made firewood of the *Mary* before they sailed. Before entering, Drake ordered all the ships to strike their topsails in honor of the Queen. Thus he acknowledged her rights in all their discoveries. Also, in honor of Master Hatton, whose crest was a golden hind, he gave the name of the *Golden Hind* to the *Pelican*. Then they entered the Straits.

Oliver always remembered the next seventeen days as a long nightmare of narrow escapes from shipwreck in twisting channels where icy winds blew from all directions. Above them, out of the darkness, rose frozen mountains. Below were deeps no cable could fathom. When at last Drake entered that ocean he had first seen from the treetop in Darien, the wind blew so hard that he could not land to set up the metal tablet claiming the country for the Queen.

Then just as the dangerous gales seemed hushed the worst one of all started to blow. They were driven in snow and darkness west and south before a storm that constantly increased in violence. The waves were like scrolls of parchment blown up from the depths, and being carried aloft were like drifts of snow blown over the tops of high mountains.

So wrote Chaplain Fletcher and added, when the *Marigold* was lost and never seen again, that some of the chief witnesses against Thomas Doughty were aboard her. He wrote that it was a judgment on them and that he heard their fearful cries as the sea overwhelmed them. Yet he himself had been one of the forty men who condemned Doughty to death.

They were blown so far south that it took until the seventh of October for the *Elizabeth* and the *Golden Hind* to reach a point slightly north of where they had left the Straits. Here Drake met Captain Wynter for the last time. He gave him a rendezvous on the coast of Peru but Wynter deserted and sailed for England.

The *Golden Hind* was now blown south again. This wind that seemed so hostile led Drake to a great discovery. Geographers had always made maps showing the Strait as a narrow passage between South America and a vast icy southern continent extending all around the globe. These maps Drake found not to be true. There was snow and ice enough on the islands they discovered, but there were wide stretches of open sea too. The Straits were not the only way into the Pacific.

The wind that had blown for fifty-two days brought them, on October 28th, to a cape extending farther towards the south than anyone had ever traveled. On this land they set up a stone with the Queen's name and the date. Oliver was with Drake when he cast himself down on the uttermost point of land and, crawling over it, reached the very tip and dipped his hands in the icy water.

When he came back to the ship, he told his crew, "I have been upon the southernmost land in the world and further southward upon it than any man yet known."

He was sure he had discovered a better way than the Straits for ships to sail around South America to China.

They sailed north-east and at last found the coast of Chile and traded in a friendly way with the natives there for fresh mutton and poultry and corn. Everything now seemed to be going well with the voyage but there soon came what to Oliver was the worst day of all. Armed only with shields and swords, they had landed to get water. More than a hundred Indians appeared and poured a shower of arrows upon the crew. Some of them hauled at the anchored boat, others snatched the oars from it. The English shields were useless at close quarters against the deadly storm of arrows.

Surf ran high. The shore was rocky. There were only two oars left in the boat when Oliver, bleeding from three wounds, swam to the boat, climbed into it, cut the painter and rowed it away from the rocks.

"Otherwise," Drake said afterwards, "all would have perished."

Oliver rowed the boat towards the wounded men floundering in the water. They were still being pierced by arrows. Drake himself was wounded under his eye as well as in his hand and arm. James had so many wounds in his right shoulder that he looked as if he had been clawed by a lion.

The boat was full of blood as they reached the ship. The chief surgeon of the fleet had died earlier in the voyage. His helper was on the *Elizabeth*. Oliver's own wounds were slight and easily cared for. He helped Drake cleanse and bind the wounds of the others but—as he said to his master—his good will was more than any skill he had. He had to cut arrows out of James's shoulder. James never made a sound. Through Drake's surgical skill, all the wounded recovered except two men.

As they sailed north, he and John Drake were often in the cabin together. Under his kinsman's direction John was making charts of the coast and painting pictures to go with the charts. Even in those days in the Straits when they could hardly tell day from night, John had made pictures that would help other ships find their way through those dark mazes. Now he had wooded hills to draw instead of snow covered rocks.

Oliver greatly admired John's skill and enjoyed looking

back over the pictures. John had a large leather-bound volume in which he had copied the best of his sketches. He painted them neatly in bright colors. There were pictures of all the ships decked out for Sundays with their gay pennants flying, of rocks covered with penguins, of dancing giants, of flying fish, of running ostriches.

John Drake also kept a journal. It was different from Master Fletcher's. The Chaplain often read especially fine passages from his aloud to anyone who would listen. John, not knowing so many fine long words and not having included any ideas for sermons, wrote briefly.

In December he noted:

Valparaiso Harbor: 35° 40'. Found all we needed—bread, bacon, wines of Chile and a great ship called the *Capitana* loaded with wine, gold and emeralds. We relieved her of her heavy burden and sailed north. Hoped to meet the *Elizabeth* but found her not.

December 20: Found a bay where we could clean and trim ship and build a pinnace. Fished for most delicate fish. Looked for our friends. Found them not.

Jan. 19, 1579. Sailed north. Jan. 22. Indians showed us watering place. Our general made them great cheer as is his manner. Came to Tarapaca. Found sleeping there a Spaniard, lying beside him thirteen bars of silver. We would not have disturbed his nap but seeing we had, we freed him from his burden so he might sleep more safely the rest of the day.

Later that same day Oliver and John Drake met an Indian boy and a Spaniard driving eight of the sheep the Peruvians call llamas.

John Drake said to Oliver, "Let us offer our services to this Spanish gentleman. I cannot bear to see him turned drover. Tell him so, Oliver."

The Spaniard scowled as Oliver spoke to him in Spanish, politely offering to drive the llamas for him.

"I need no help," the Spaniard answered.

He pushed his hat down on his head, slung his cloak over one shoulder and thrust his chin forward, then raised the stick he had been using to herd the llamas as if he meant to strike Oliver with it.

Oliver did not move. He said gently, "No doubt the señor sees the ship below us in the harbor and the boats coming ashore? And the man standing ready to land? See, he jumps to the beach. That, señor, is Francisco Draque—"

The Spaniard did not stay to hear more. Dropping his stick he started running. The wind blew both his cloak and his hat off.

"He must have remembered something he meant to do," Oliver said, picking up the stick.

The Indian boy stood staring after his master but did not follow him. He spoke to the llamas which were crowding together. They formed in line again. With the boy's help Oliver and John drove them to the beach near the boats. Each llama was saddled with two leather bags full of silver, eight hundred pounds in all.

Drake was pleased with the silver, the llamas were glad to get rid of their loads, the Indian boy was delighted with a knife, a whistle and an English cap of red wool, and John Drake was happy with a new picture to draw. He gave it to Oliver who laughed every time he looked at the haughty Spanish gentleman, bounding off like a scared rabbit at the name of Francisco Draque.

John wrote in his diary:

Jan. 26. The Spaniards gave us llamas. They are the height and length of a pretty cow. Upon their backs can sit three men and a boy. They have necks like camels, heads like sheep. Their flesh is good meat, wool is fine and they are good carriers going over mountains with marvelous loads.

Feb. 7. Entered Arica. In two barks found forty bars of silver, like bricks, 20 pounds each.

Feb. 9. On our way to Lima met bark with some silver and gold and another loaded with linen. Took both.

Feb. 15. Arrived at Lima. In its harbor, called Callao, were thirty ships. We entered at night and anchored in the midst of them. Still hoped to find *Elizabeth* and *Marigold*, trusting she had been saved from storm, so we did not attack the Spanish ships. We heard through Indians we had brought with us, of the ship of Miguel Angelo that had much plate, besides silk, linen and coin. Also of one they called the *Cacafuego* (spitfire) of San Juan de Anton, which had left Feb. 2 for Panama. So after cutting cables of all ships in the harbor, we set sail (Feb. 16) the pinnace towing us when the wind failed, in pursuit of the *Cacafuego*. Feb. 24. Passed Guayaquil. Feb. 28. Crossed Equator.

March 1. Passed Cape Francisco. Saw a sail.

Drake had not left Callao without being noticed. Bells were ringing as he left the tangle of drifting ships. The Governor of Lima had hurried from the city to the port and had ordered soldiers into two ships to pursue the pirate. The wind fell to a dead calm. Even with every sail set and the men in the pinnace sweating at the oars to tow her, the *Golden Hind* barely moved over the glassy sea.

Still, the Spanish ships were in worse case. They had no large guns and were without ballast so they could carry little sail. All day in the glaring heat they labored after Drake but by evening they had almost lost sight of him. They had no provisions. Many of the cavaliers were so seasick they could not stand, much less fight. Seeing they could do nothing against the enemy if they caught him, they became less and less anxious to meet him. They went back to Lima.

There they were in more danger than at sea. The angry viceroy, Drake's old enemy, Martin Enríquez, had some of them hanged and rebuked them all for cowardice. Then he ordered guns cast to arm ships for a new pursuit. In the meantime a breeze sprang up and the *Golden Hind* dashed ahead. The breeze became a gale and the distance between her and the *Cacafuego* shortened. Drake sailed in the pinnace close inshore. The *Golden Hind* moved in line with him half a league out to sea.

They captured a frigate and learned from her that the *Cacafuego* was not far ahead. Drake offered a gold chain to the man who first saw the sails of the rich prize. John Drake was first up the mast and before long he called down, claiming the chain. Soon all could see her. There she was, the *Cacafuego*, sailing quietly along to seaward.

It was only noon. Drake did not wish to attack before dark. He knew that to reduce sail might arouse suspicion on the *Cacafuego*. He ordered some wine jars trailed at the stern of the *Golden Hind* and of the pinnace to reduce speed and to deceive the Spanish ship about his power of sailing.

It was eight o'clock before San Juan de Anton, owner and captain of the *Cacafuego*, began to wonder about the two ships behind him and farther inshore. They hardly seemed to move yet they still plodded along not far away. Perhaps, he thought, the viceroy is sending me some message.

He came about suddenly and sailed towards the *Golden Hind*. Drake in the pinnace at once had the drag cut away. The master of the *Golden Hind* did the same thing. At nine o'clock the pinnace passed astern of the *Cacafuego* and came alongside her.

Anton hailed the pinnace.

He was answered by voices shouting, "English! English! Strike sail!"

Then a single voice, louder than the others cried, "Strike sail, señor San Juan de Anton, unless you wish to be sent to the bottom."

"Strike!" cried Anton. "What kind of a cruet stand do you think this is to strike! Come aboard and do it yourselves!"

He was answered by a whistle, a trumpet call and a volley of shot and arrows. They came both from the pinnace on his port side and the other ship to starboard. He tried in vain to sail away. A shot from a big gun sent his mizzenmast overboard. A hailstorm of shot and arrows made it impossible to repair the damage. His men fled below. Forty English poured over the side. Resistance was hopeless. He surrendered and, with his passengers and officers, was rowed to the *Golden Hind.*

The man who had led the English on board the *Cacafuego* was already on his own deck. He was a short ruddy bearded man with very blue eyes. He was taking off his helmet and breastplate.

He said gently, putting his hand on Anton's shoulder, "Accept with patience what is the usage of war."

It was with Anton as it had been with other captains along that coast. He could not believe that there were English in the Pacific. It was a Spanish ocean. The Pope had drawn a line down the middle of the world and had given everything east of it to Portugal and everything west of it to Spain.

So Spain had the West Indies and Portugal had the East Indies. Unfortunately, the Pope's generous intentions towards

Spain were better than his knowledge of geography. He had thought the world smaller than it really was. He meant to give Spain all South America but he had drawn the line too far west, so he had accidentally given Brazil to Portugal. However, Anton felt, this was only temporary. King Philip, he thought, would surely get Brazil away from the Portuguese and musical Castilian would be spoken there.

Yet the English had dared to enter King Philip's ocean and here he was, San Juan de Anton, prisoner in the cabin of an English ship, guarded by twelve Englishmen, some of them as tall as Patagonians. Anton had lived in London at one time so he spoke some English. Also some of them spoke Spanish. There was a tall young page—Oliver, they called him—who spoke Spanish well, only with a Cadiz accent. His nurse came from Cadiz, he told Anton.

He treated Anton with courtesy, bringing him food in a silver dish, carrying the meat neatly and tasting it politely to show it was not poisoned. Anton and the other Spaniards were all amazed by the treatment they received. They found it hard to believe that the man off whose silver plates they were eating was the terrible pirate, Francisco Draque, whose name in Nombre de Dios was used to frighten little boys so that they woke up screaming. Draque was supposed to be seven feet tall with fierce black eyes and a knife in his teeth. He skinned people alive and ate them raw. This unpleasant character was not much like the quiet man who would come across from Anton's ship to listen to music after supper.

Oliver learned Spanish airs from one of the passengers and played them on the cittern, and John Drake, with his gold chain around his neck, danced for their pleasure.

They sailed out to sea for two nights and a day till Drake

felt sure he was far enough from trade routes to make it safe to transfer the *Cacafuego*'s cargo to the *Golden Hind*. The pinnace brought load after load. There were thirteen chests of pieces of eight and eighty pounds of gold. There were jewels—great emeralds, handfuls of pearls. There was gold and silver plate. There were twenty-six tons of silver bars. They threw out the *Golden Hind's* ballast and used silver in its place.

The only time Anton saw Drake angry was when Drake heard what had happened to John Oxenham, his friend who had hoped to sail the Pacific with him. Oxenham was on a voyage to the Spanish Main so he had not sailed with Drake. He had fallen into the hands of Don Martin Enriquez and had been executed.

Drake said hotly with his hand on his sword, "Tell Don Martin Enríquez to hang no more English or he will receive from me a present of two thousand Spanish heads."

The prisoners turned pale but he hurt no one. Indeed, as Anton said afterwards, he treated them with great kindness. He gave Anton a gilt corselet and a fine German firelock. All the Spanish officers received gifts and to each of the crew he gave money and clothing. Their ship was returned to them in good condition.

As he was leaving, Anton asked Drake how he expected to get the treasure home. Drake showed him on a large chart, which he said he bought in Lisbon for eight hundred ducats, three possible ways for his journey. One was by the Moluccas, the East Indies and the Cape of Good Hope. Another was by the way he had come. He had passed the Straits of Magellan once and could again. The third was by a northern passage that would bring them to Norway. There was also a fourth, he said, but he did not name it. This fourth way was by the southernmost cape with the open water around it. The English kept the secret so well that it was many years before the Spaniards heard about it. Even then they did not know that Drake had been there first. Anton believed that Drake meant to cross the isthmus at Panama, seize a ship and go home by the West Indies.

The *Golden Hind* was sailing north when he last saw her.

LONG VOYAGE

Don Francisco Zarate was bound for Peru with a cargo of silk, porcelain and other goods from China. On the fourth of April the steersman was the only man awake on deck. Suddenly he saw, looming against the moon, a large ship. It would run him down in a moment. Her crew must be asleep, he thought.

"Haul clear! Haul clear!" he shouted.

There was no answer.

"What ship are you?" he called.

A voice in Spanish said, "The ship of Miguel Angelo."

The stranger was towing a smaller vessel, which, as they passed, swung close to Zarate's ship. There was a volley of small shot. Men swarmed over the rail calling for the Spaniards to surrender. Zarate now came on deck. So safe was the Pacific, King Philip's private ocean, that he thought it was all a joke. The surprise was so complete that he could only surrender without resistance. No violence was offered to him or the other prisoners. They were asked politely for their swords and keys.

Zarate was escorted on board the *Golden Hind* by a tall young man who spoke good Spanish.

Drake was pacing her deck.

I went up to him and kissed his hands [Zarate wrote in his report to the viceroy]. He received me with a good countenance and took me to his cabin where he said, "I am a very good friend to those who deal with me truly but to those who do not—And so you shall tell me, for this is the way to stand well with me, what gold or silver that ship carries."

I replied, "none." He repeated the question. "None," I answered, "only one or two plates on which I am served and one or two cups and that is all."

He remained silent a while and then asked if I knew Don Martin Enríquez. I said I knew Your Excellency and he asked if any relation of yours or anything belonging to you was with me. I said no and he went on, "Because I would rather meet with him than with all the gold in the Indies, that I might show him how to keep the word of a gentleman." I made no reply.

Drake had me sit next to him at dinner and helped me from his own dish. He is served on silver dishes with gilded garlands in which are his arms. He carries all possible dainties and scents. Many of these things were given him by the Queen. None of his gentlemen took a seat or covered his head until repeatedly urged by Drake. They are called to dinner by trumpets and clarions and they dine to the music of viols. None of his men dared take anything from my ship without his orders.

He assured me that my life and ship were safe. Water, he said, was what he wanted. He spoke much of the death of a friend of his called Thomas Doughty, who had committed mutinous acts touching the Queen's service. He showed me her instructions. Doughty was tried and beheaded at Port St Julian.

The dead man's brother was on the ship. He dined at Drake's table but did not speak nor did others speak to him. He never left the ship as others did. I inquired of the crew if Drake had private enemies but I heard of none. All agreed that their general, as they call him, was adored.

The day after our capture was Sunday. Drake dressed himself handsomely and ordered his galleon trimmed with all the streamers and flags he had. He spent most of the day in overhauling my ship. What he took from me was not much. He took certain pieces of Chinese porcelain and begged me to excuse him, saying they were for his wife. He gave me in exchange a curved dagger and a silver chafing dish. For his courtesy, I gave him a gold falcon with spread wings and with a jewel in its breast.

He thanked me and said, "You shall go tomorrow when the sea breeze rises." So next day he gave back our keys and rapiers. To all sailors and to the poorer passengers he gave a handful of silver coins.

His ship is a very good galleon, as well mounted with artillery as any I have seen in my life. His crew is about a hundred men of warlike age, the rest craftsmen and boys. I believe no vessel can overtake him.

I think [Zarate ended his report] he is the greatest sailor who ever lived.

Philip II of Spain, ruler of the greatest empire in the world, was probably the hardest working man in it. He loved shady gardens with fountains and orange trees, but he spent most of the day and much of the night in a cramped bare room reading dispatches about his empire. Often they were written in handwriting difficult to read. The light by which he worked was often dim. His eyes were red-rimmed with weariness. He ate and drank and slept little. He wore the same black clothes from year to year. They were worn at the elbows from writing and at the knees from praying. He had no friends, only servants and courtiers. He saw little of his family. His room in the Escorial, a monastery built like a fortress on a lonely mountain, was more like a monk's cell than the apartment of a king.

Here Philip planned how to make more of the world, especially England, part of his empire and here he studied everything that touched this enterprise. When reports about Drake's activities in the Pacific began to come in, King Philip must have slept less than ever.

Fleets—he read—were being sent in search of the pirate. Treasure was being kept ashore instead of being shipped to Panama. Forts were being built to protect it. Rivers were closed with chains against the corsair's fleet, which was of various sizes according to the imagination of the writer. Bishops were having church bells melted and cast into cannon. More and more money was needed. Estimates of the gold and silver Drake had taken grew larger and larger.

The bills for expenses were not only for the Pacific Coast. War galleys and galiots hunted for the corsair on the Atlantic side of the isthmus. Bronze cannon, muskets, arquebuses and pikes were being collected all along the Spanish Main. Guatemala, Cartagena and Nicaragua were just as active and expensive to King Philip as Lima and Panama.

He read many opinions, all different, about which way

Drake would go home. He had said he would go by a northern strait to Norway or else by the Moluccas and the Cape of Good Hope. Of course, he would lie about it. Wise men, especially the kind of cavalier who was easily sick at sea, said he would seize Panama, cross the isthmus and seize ships to carry him and his hundreds of tons of treasure across the Atlantic. Others thought he would winter on the coast of California and then sail south, robbing ports as he went, and go home through the Straits. So all ports and the Straits must be fortified. Citizens must be warned of his coming. Plans must be made to catch him in the Straits.

Drake in the meantime was quietly sailing north along the coast of California. He was hoping to find a strait around North America. By June 3rd they were in latitude 42° north. The weather had been warm but suddenly one night John Drake wrote—there was bitter nipping cold.

Dawn brought no relief. Rain froze as it fell, ropes grew stiff. So pinched and numb were the crew they could hardly sail the ship. Yet still our General hauled on the ropes himself and urged us on, thinking such cold must be unusual and temporary. Next day the wind was more cruel than ever. It blew from the north-west and forced us to anchor close to shore. We were tossed by violent squalls and stifled by most vile thick fogs. We still tried to run north and find the strait but a gale carried us back past a coast where hills were covered with snow. We found a good harbor and anchored there.

At last Drake decided to give up the search for a northern strait and to sail home round the Cape of Good Hope. On

July 23rd they put out to sea. The Indians, with whom he had made friends, crowded the hilltops, making fires as if to beg them to return.

Oliver always remembered how Drake looked as he said, "That coast may well come under the rule of our own Queen and English be spoken there someday."

They were out of sight of land for sixty-eight days. On September 30th they reached some islands near the Equator. The inhabitants came out to welcome them in finely decorated canoes and proved to be so handy at stealing that Drake called the place the Isle of Thieves. It was not until October 21st that they found an island where they could safely anchor and get water.

At last on November 3rd Oliver, who was at the mast head, saw the cones of the famous Spice Islands rising from the sea. They visited one called Ternate. Four war canoes, hung with costly mats, rowed to the sound of music, carrying men of the Sultan's court, came out to receive them. The Sultan followed in state. On the deck of the *Golden Hind* he said he would value an alliance with Queen Elizabeth and would grant her a monopoly of the spice trade in his dominions.

> This Sultan [John Drake wrote] was a tall stout man of kingly and gracious countenance. His people were dressed in fine white cloth or calico. He wore cloth of gold from his waist down. On his feet were shoes of scarlet leather; on his head rings of gold an inch wide rather like a crown. He had a thick chain of gold around his neck. On his left hand were rings of emerald, diamond, ruby. On his right diamond and turquoise. His page stood at his right and

moved a fan, richly embroidered and set with sapphires, to keep him cool.

The *Golden Hind* fired a salute in the Sultan's honor. Her trumpets sounded and she was towed into the harbor by the war canoes. Drake ordered his musicians into a boat to escort the Sultan's canoe. Oliver and the others played English airs as they went. The Sultan listened to every note and when they paused, kept calling to them in Portuguese to go on.

They spent four days at Ternate loading spices and provisions. Before they left, Drake and the Sultan signed a treaty about the spice trade. They sailed on towards Celebes, stopping at an island nearby to clean and repair their ship.

They called it their Earthly Paradise. They lived there a month, with food they needed for the picking, breathing the softest air. There were fifty-six men now in the crew, all as well and strong as when they left England. They needed that strength, for the next weeks were full of contrary winds and violent storms, straits not shown on their charts, twisting passages. On January 9th, 1580, they thought they were free and clear but they ran on a shoal three or four leagues long. For hours they expected that at any minute the ship would split to pieces. The best they could hope for was to be cast away on one of the wild islands they had passed.

Drake cheerfully told them to hearten up and ordered them to lighten the ship by throwing out some of the spices they had bought in Ternate. Oliver helped to throw out three tons of cloves, precious as silver, but she did not move.

Chaplain Fletcher preached one of his long sermons at this time. Oliver had long ago given up listening to the chaplain's sermons and he did not remember a word of this one after it was over. He was too busy helping to throw out guns, food and enough silver for a king's ransom. Still the *Golden Hind* did not float and about four in the afternoon she slowly heeled over. All knew now that the end was near. They had no shred of hope left. Yet, to the amazement of all, she suddenly floated free and slid off into deep water.

Just how the chaplain had offended Drake during those dark hours, Oliver never knew. Neither did John Drake. If the other officers knew, they never told. Had the chaplain in one of his dark bursts of oratory spoken the name of Thomas Doughty and called their peril God's vengeance for his death? Or had he tried to rouse the men against Drake? All Oliver knew was that when the ship was safely at sea, the trumpets sounded and the whole crew came together on the deck. There Drake seated himself in judgment and ordered the chaplain's leg fettered and the fetter fastened by a padlock to the hatch.

Then he said sternly, "Francis Fletcher, I do here excommunicate thee out of the Church of God and from all the benefits and graces thereof, and do denounce thee to the Devil and all his angels."

He forbade Fletcher to come before the mast on pain of death and swore that he would be hanged if he did. He ordered these words written on a paper and the paper bound around Fletcher's arm: "Francis Fletcher, the falsest knave that liveth."

Fletcher was then unfettered but there were no more sermons from him on that voyage. James was especially pleased with this change. The chaplain had tried hard to convert him, with the result that James was stauncher than ever in the Catholic faith.

Their dangers were not over. For a month they beat about among islands that loomed before them whichever way they turned. At last, by the help of some native pilots, they got clear and sailed for Java. On March 11th they were received by a friendly rajah. They cleaned ship once more, traded for food and for spices to replace those cast into the sea, and on March 26th sailed for the Cape of Good Hope and England.

It was Sunday the 26th of September, 1580, when they arrived at Plymouth, they thought. Oliver pictured it as it was when Drake came back from Nombre de Dios. The church bells would ring, people would come running out of the church and gather on Plymouth Hoe, shouting and waving as the *Golden Hind* sailed from the end of the world into Plymouth Harbor.

None of this happened.

It was Monday!

COUNCIL DOOR

As they sailed westwards all those months a day had slipped away from them. It was, Oliver thought, like the sound of the music they had played—on Patagonian beaches, in the icy straits while the wind howled, in the green shade of tropical islands, even that morning in Plymouth Harbor—gone, no one knew where or how.

The lost day was not the only strange thing about their return. Drake had anxiously asked the first fishermen they met about the Queen, for her health and strength meant much to him as they did to all England. There had been plots against her life but she was alive and well, thank God, they said. But a great plague was raging in Plymouth. They advised Drake to anchor in the harbor and not to go into the town. So he anchored and his wife came out in a boat to welcome him. So did the Mayor of Plymouth. From them he heard news that made him leave the harbor and anchor behind an island in the sound.

They told Drake that Captain Wynter had been well received when he returned to England. Wynter told how he had passed through the Straits of Magellan but had returned because of the furious weather, he said. Drake, he added, had disappeared in a violent gale. He made it sound as if Drake had deserted him rather than the other way. Certainly those who heard him never expected to see Drake again. Wynter reported Doughty's execution but was ordered to say no more about it till Drake came home—if he ever did.

In the meantime it was rumored that Philip II was preparing a great fleet to conquer England. The Queen's counselors, especially the Treasurer, Lord Burghley, and the city merchants of London were anxious to keep on good terms with Spain. If Philip was angered by what Drake was doing in the Indies, the merchants were afraid they would find themselves looking into the mouths of guns belonging to tall Spanish galleons.

It was not until the summer of 1579 that Philip learned that Drake was in the Pacific. His voyage was still a secret in England. Even after Wynter came home it was believed that Drake had been shipwrecked in the Straits. The first news that he was very much alive came to England from Spain after Philip began receiving reports of what Drake had done.

The story lost nothing in the telling. Pilots and such skilled mariners as Anton and Zarate had made accurate reports of Drake's seizure of their ships and of his courteous treatment of them, but with the landsmen it was different. They had invented a whole fleet of English ships and battles that never took place. Monks and inquisitors knew more details than anyone, especially about murdered and tortured Spaniards. These stories had come to England through the Spanish ambassador. They had even been repeated to Mistress Drake by people who should have known better, she considered.

"I told them," she said, "that you never tortured anyone or killed anyone except in a fair fight."

Drake said mildly, "I did duck one Spaniard from the yard-arm because he would not answer a question I asked him. He was quite dry, I think, when I sent him ashore."

Mistress Drake laughed and said, "But you did shoot a cannon ball at me. Everyone in Devon knows it."

"A cannon ball!" Drake exclaimed.

"Yes," the mayor said, laughing. "All Plymouth saw it."

They told him the story, both talking at once as Oliver served them their dinner.

When Mistress Drake's family heard Captain Wynter's report that Drake's ship had vanished in a furious storm, they began, she said, to treat her like a widow. By the end of the year they had found a respectable well-to-do landowner who was willing to marry her.

"Doubtless a kind and courteous gentleman and one you liked well? I hope..." Drake said.

"I did not like him at all," said his wife, "but what could I do? Every day it was the same thing. They'd say, 'You are a widow, alone in the world, who will protect you? No one.' After some months I began to believe it."

"She was wrong," the Mayor put in. "As we found out at the church."

Mistress Drake took a sip of tea—Oliver had learned to make it in Ternate—out of one of Don Francisco Zarate's porcelain cups. It was gray-green porcelain with plum blossoms painted on it.

"So at last they persuaded me and I went to the church. My bridegroom looked so respectable I could scarce forbear casting my prayer book at him."

"What did you do instead?" Drake asked.

"I cried."

"But she dried her eyes," the Mayor said, "and they were just upon entering the church when—"

"I heard a sound of powder roaring and a great cannon ball burst up from the earth between us! I cried out, 'It's from Drake to tell me he is still alive. He forbids this marriage. I'll have none but Frankie Drake for my husband,' I said. 'Take back your ring, sir,' I said to the bridegroom, for he had given me a ring with a mean pearl and a few sparks of diamond in it! So I handed it to him and put my prayer book under my arm and picked up my cannon ball. I have it at home."

It was many months since Oliver had heard Drake laugh as he did then.

"I'll have it plated with gold and set some sparks of diamonds in it and some pearls, big ones," he said to his wife when he could speak. "What was it?" he said to the Mayor. "A spent ball from gunnery practice?"

"Yes," said the Mayor. "The gunner was severely spoken to, I promise you."

"You should have given him a medal," Drake said.

"Nonsense," said Mistress Drake. "It came straight through the whole world to my feet. You shall see it soon."

It was a long time before Drake saw it.

"The London merchants," the Mayor told Drake, "say that if you have brought home any gold or silver, it must be registered, every ounce of it, and returned to the King of Spain. He is already busy stirring up rebellion in Ireland in revenge for what you have done. The merchants fear that their ships will be seized in Spanish ports and their captains will be put on the rack by the inquisitors. The Queen has sent you a message by me. She says that she has heard of the great robberies you have committed and that every peso must be returned."

Drake's answer was to send John Brewer to London to see Master Hatton—Sir Christopher now—and to tell him what the ship, named in his honor, had done. Oliver went with the trumpeter. They left Oliver's viols and cittern and Brewer's trumpet on the *Golden Hind*. They did, however, take with them such things as might interest a woman, even a queen: a cup of green porcelain, some emeralds as long as her little finger, a few large pearls, some cloth of gold from Tidore.

Sir Christopher Hatton was a knight of the Garter now and one of the Queen's most trusted counselors. He had always treated Brewer with kindness and his gentle friendly manner had not changed. He remembered Oliver.

"Why, you are the boy who brought the lute to the Queen at Kenilworth!" he said. "And now you're as tall as a Patagonian, I swear."

"I'm only six foot two—and it was more of a cittern really," Oliver said.

Sir Christopher listened to all that Brewer had to tell him, asking many questions, especially about Thomas Doughty. They did not see the Queen but Hatton had audience with her, showed her the presents Drake had sent and gave Brewer a message to carry back to Plymouth.

They rode as fast as they could to tell Drake that the Queen summoned him to court, desired him to bring with him some of the curiosities he had collected on his travels and said that he should fear nothing. As soon as Brewer and Oliver got back to Plymouth with the message, Drake put the silver ballast of the *Golden Hind* and most of the gold into the hands of a local magistrate for safekeeping. He then set off for London with several horseloads of gold and jewels.

Oliver, John Drake, James Campion and John Brewer went with him. In London, Drake bought them new clothes with the latest thing in slashes and laces and ruffs. He himself chose plain dark blue English cloth which differed from his usual dress only by having no salt-water stains on it. He was the shortest and most plainly dressed of the group but no one on the streets looked at anyone else.

The city merchants were angry with him. Mendoza, the Spanish ambassador, was threatening war and calling Drake a pirate and a murderer. Lord Burghley, the Treasurer, said that all Spanish gold must be returned and Drake punished. Other counselors, some of whom had pensions from the King of Spain, passed an order saying the same thing. The people on the streets felt differently. Drake walked as proudly in his plain clothes as if he were on the deck of his own ship calling on a Spaniard to surrender, and the people of London cheered him as he went by.

The Queen and Sir Christopher Hatton were in a council meeting when Drake came to the Palace. Master Laneham was keeping the council door. He tripped briskly up to Drake and invited him to sit on a bench beside him while he waited. Master Laneham was handsomely dressed in brown silk with an enormous wired ruff that kept his sharp chin and nose pointing upward. His bright eyes twinkled at Oliver and he said, "Why, our lad who brought the cittern has become a giant, I vow! And the singer too—we have no dolphin big enough to hold you both!"

Oliver was pleased that Master Laneham remembered that the cittern was not a lute. He and James were both getting tired of being called giants.

James muttered angrily, "The next little cock sparrow that calls me a giant, I'll pick him up and throw him into the Thames, I swear."

"I'll come and visit you in the Tower," Oliver said.

Master Laneham said to Drake, "Now when the door opens, Her Majesty will come through it first. You must all kneel where she can see you well, yet you must not be in her way, nor yet too far back or she may go past without noticing you. Her Majesty walks swiftly, and especially on a day when she is not pleased with her council. Sometimes she boxes the ears of anyone who crowds too close. Let us ponder a moment—yes. Master Drake had better kneel here, and the others behind him, the two young giants on the ends, please."

James growled at this point and Oliver said soothingly, "Quiet! You're just a Patagonian dwarf."

Master Laneham went on, "Yes, that looks well. Now when you kneel, do not thump down like sacks of flour but sink gracefully to your knees, the right knee first, taking off your hats and holding them against your hearts. Bow your heads as the door opens, then raise them, looking up at the Queen's Grace, and say 'Cheese'."

"Cheese? What foolery is this?" Drake asked angrily.

"Not out loud, of course," Master Laneham explained patiently. "Merely with the tongue of inner speech. It gives a most pleasant expression to the lips."

He went on to say that it was especially desirable to have a pleasant expression today since it was not, he feared, one of Her Majesty's good days. It was not necessary to listen at the keyhole to tell that, he said.

Indeed it was not. They could hear a shrill voice. It was like an angry peacock's on the terrace at Campions', Oliver thought.

Could this be the Queen—who had spoken so gently in the garden at Kenilworth?

Oliver had heard fishwives on a wharf at Boston screaming at each other in much the same tones. As he stood there in the gallery hung with splendid tapestries where knights hunted the unicorn in flowery fields, he felt more homesick for the sight of Boston Stump than while hauling on an icy rope in the Straits or thirsting for fresh water on the coast of Chile.

James felt differently.

"I wish I were in Patagonia," he groaned. He pulled his new plumed hat down over his eyes and, scowling under the velvet brim, added, "Chasing ostriches."

Just then there was a final burst of fishwife screams from the council chamber. The door was hastily flung open.

Oliver thought, Now comes the hurricane! and thumped down on his knees. As he snatched off his hat he heard James say, "Cheddar!" which is—as James stated afterwards—a kind of cheese. Saying it, however, does not produce an especially amiable look. Unfortunately, James was beside Oliver, thus unbalancing Master Laneham's carefully posed picture, and Brewer, whose legs were still stiff from many arrow wounds, could hardly kneel at all. When James dragged off his hat, his straight reddish-gold hair stood up like a wheat field reviving after a heavy rain. He had his hat clutched to his stomach. His face was as red as the roses among which the unicorn was leaping.

Oliver, James said afterwards, had turned the color of a seasick Spaniard.

The hurricane, Oliver thought, was cloudy purple. It flashed gold lightning with little flames of emerald and ruby. He had forgotten to raise his head. He saw only a long fingered very

white hand against the purple and a sleeve embroidered with butterflies.

Then the voice he remembered from the garden at Kenilworth said, "Why, Drake, it is you!"

Oliver looked up.

Master Drake was kissing the Queen's hand and she was looking down at him with great kindness.

"Come!" she said. "We have much to talk of."

Drake got to his feet as nimbly as if all he ever did for a day's work was to kneel on Turkey carpets. His followers did not see him again for six hours. In those hours Drake must have convinced the Queen that Philip II's charges that Drake had murdered Spanish subjects were false. She had told Mendoza, Philip's ambassador, that she would not decide about the treasure until she had heard Drake's answer to the accusations against him.

Now, she told Mendoza, she had no reason to believe that Drake had injured any of Philip's subjects, but she had ordered the treasure registered so that it might be returned if justice so demanded.

Mendoza was furious. He began to threaten war against England and demanded that Drake's head should be cut off. The Queen's reply was that not a penny of the treasure would be returned until every Spanish soldier had left Ireland where they were stirring up bloody revolutions and killing her subjects.

Drake, in the meantime, was once more on the road to Plymouth. The Queen allowed him to keep ten thousand pounds of the treasure for himself and generous sums for the crew. There was still a long train of pack horses that carried the rest of it to London where it was lodged in the Tower for safekeeping.

It was a dark, short, chilly day, like a June day in Patagonia,

Oliver thought. Smoke rose from the chimneys of London. It was blacker than the smoke made by the giants when they were trying to wreck strange ships. Yet the people of London lined the streets to see the pack horses as if they were waiting for the Queen herself. Their cheers for Drake were like the roar of waves against icy rocks in the straits. The Tower, rising out of the smoky fog, was like some tower of ice against which their ship might be cast.

Before long Drake's ship was sailing in smoother waters. The Queen had ordered him, before he paid off his crew, to have the *Golden Hind* sailed into the Thames and anchored at Deptford where not only she herself but all London could see that brave ship.

Now even the London merchants forgot their hostility to Drake.

Mendoza wrote to his master, "Drake has returned to court where he passes much time with the Queen and is told how great is his service to her."

On April 4th, 1581, the Queen went to Deptford to visit the *Golden Hind*. She took with her the Sieur de Marchaumont. The Duc d' Alençon, heir to the throne of France, was courting her at this time. Marchaumont was his special envoy. Mendoza wrote to Philip of Spain that the banquet served on board Drake's ship was finer than anything seen in England since the time of Henry VIII.

Oliver and James and John Drake, who helped serve it, were bewildered by the number of dishes. There was mutton cooked like venison, veal and ham pies, chicken pies, roast swans and geese, skylarks and snipes, salmon, sturgeon and eels. There were custards that took fifty eggs to make and a great pie of preserved quinces with gilt pastry. Smythsonne,

Queen Elizabeth's master cook, had sent a wonderful cake made of crushed almonds and sugar and white of egg. It was called a marchpane and it was molded in the shape of the Tower of London where the treasure still lay.

"But where is the salted seal meat?" James asked as he and Oliver ran into each other on the way to the galley. "And the moldy biscuit with weevils in it? And the green water? There's no nourishment in gilt pastry. I don't feel at home."

Things were not all changed on the *Golden Hind*. She was hung with banners and streamers as she had been on Sundays at sea and there was music after dinner. Oliver played his viol da gamba. James sang old songs that the Queen knew—"Pastime with Good Company," a song of Henry VIII's, was one of them.

After the singing, John Drake did his morris dance, leaping higher than ever, Oliver thought, as he played the cittern for him.

The Queen spoke to them all kindly and gave them her hand to kiss.

She said to Oliver, "But your cittern is not so fine as mine. I was playing it only yesterday."

"Your Majesty would make this one sound better," Oliver said, holding it out, but she only slapped the strings lightly with a hand covered with emeralds which had traveled half around the world and said, "We have other things to do even pleasanter than music."

She called Drake to her and said, "Kneel down, Drake. The King of Spain has asked for your head. I must strike it off."

She was holding a gilded sword which she handed to the Sieur de Marchaumont. He used it to touch Drake on the shoulder but it was her voice that rang out: "Rise, Sir Francis Drake, master thief of the unknown world."

Mendoza thought that the Queen had given the sword to Marchaumont to show that England was now allied with France against Spain and that she would marry d'Alençon. She did not marry this ugly young man half her age, whom she called her Frog, but she pretended that she would with so much success that King Philip must have slept poorly in his narrow cell in the Escorial.

She ordered the *Golden Hind* hauled ashore at Deptford. One admirer of Drake's suggested that the ship ought to be raised up and set on the stump of the steeple of St. Paul's. The top of the steeple had been struck by lightning and burnt down. However, the Queen merely had a hole dug for the ship and a shed built over her.

Oliver did not see the *Golden Hind* in her new position. Long before the hole was ready he was back in Boston. He learned about the ship from a letter with pictures in it from John Drake.

The shed is high enough [John wrote] so her lower masts are left standing. As for the main mast, it is laid down and scholars from Winchester School have composed Latin verses in Sir F. Drake's honor and have cut them in the wood. He swears he will learn Latin and read them. The shed is a hundred and eighty feet long and twenty-four wide. Parties from London have dinner on board. Sir F. says he will set up as tavern keeper to earn his living if needs must.

John Doughty accused Sir F. of his brother's murder. The judges heard the case but nothing came of it. Now it is discovered that John Doughty has been plotting to kill Drake (I forget to say Sir Francis—do you?) with a Spaniard called Zubiaur. Sir C. Hatton has discovered that King Philip offers 20,000 ducats to anyone who will kidnap Drake and bring the King his head. I wonder who is brave enough! Not J. Doughty, I think, even if he were not in prison for these doings.

John Drake had drawn a picture of the *Golden Hind* as she would look on top of St. Paul's steeple and another one of Drake serving beer to thirsty customers on her deck.
He also wrote about the latest plot against the Queen's life.

One man has confessed that he was ready to stab her, had his hand on his knife indeed. Then she looked at him. Her look made him think of King Harry and he ran away but as James sings:

> *The hunt is up, the hunt is up*
> *And it is well nigh day.*
> *And Harry our King has gone hunting*
> *To bring the deer to bay.*

They have caught this timid stabber and he, at least, will put his hand on his dagger no more and so let it be with all the Queen's enemies.

Yours,
J. DRAKE

PRINTER'S INK

It began to seem to Oliver that he would never see Boston Stump again, yet the day came at last.

Not long after Drake was knighted the crew of the *Golden Hind* was paid off. It was as Drake had promised them. The poorest had enough money to buy an estate and be a country gentleman. Not many did. Sir Francis himself settled down in Devon and became Mayor of Plymouth. He interested himself in getting a supply of fresh water for the town. He did not have his wife's cannon ball plated with gold. She liked it as it was, she said, and she would show it to visitors and tell the story.

A few of the crew also went back to their own towns, but most of them were too restless for life in the country. Their talk was all of new ventures on the Spanish Main, of making their gold bring them more gold—and more—heaps of it, topped off with emeralds and pearls. Every stay-at-home Londoner who had risked one pound on the voyage had got back forty-seven pounds. The next one would be even better, they told each other wisely when they met in taverns.

Some of the sailors spent all they had while they talked about it. Others talked too loudly and were robbed. Some bought taverns so they could have a place to talk about the voyage for the rest of their lives whether anyone listened or not. Others ventured their money on voyages and sailed either east or west. Some of them were captured by the Spaniards before they ever sailed the Pacific.

James was one of the restless ones, but he went home with Oliver before he went to sea again. He wanted to see Isabel, he said. They both expected to see her riding a black horse along the Campions' road. She would be taller, they agreed, and would dance better than ever. So would Joyce, Oliver said. James stated that his twin would be six foot four—he was, wasn't he?—and dance like a Patagonian. She would be freckled too, he said.

He was wrong.

They did not see Isabel on the road that led past Campions'. It was a hot May afternoon as they ended their journey. A big lumbering coach had left them at a dusty crossroads. They were glad to find themselves in the dancing shade of arched elms they both remembered. The elms made a long green tunnel. At the end of it they could see a curve of the River Witham and above it Boston Stump with great thunderheads rising behind it.

To their left they saw rose-red brick and clipped yews.

"Campions'," James said.

They stopped and looked up the roadway that led to the house. Grass grew thickly on it. The iron gates were locked and chained and rusty.

They looked at each other without speaking.

"Gone to Ireland perhaps for a visit," Oliver said at last.

James said, "The elephant hasn't been clipped for a year—or more."

They trudged on in silence. Their cloak-bags grew heavier at each step. Where the elms ended and the sunshine blazed on the thatched roofs of the manor farm, James set down his cloak-bag and mopped his face.

"I meant to use my ostrich feathers to have a fan made for her," he said gloomily. "Green and white."

"So did I," said Oliver, "red and white."

"Green," James said, but with so little spirit that Oliver did not even answer.

Their silence was broken by a familiar sound—the click of the farm gate shutting close to them. A slender not very tall girl had just come through it. The sun made reddish lights in her bright gold hair. She had a basket of eggs in one hand and a plump fowl with the feathers still on in the other.

Oliver had just time to see that she had no more than three freckles on her nose before she dropped both basket and fowl and came running up to James. She did not run like any Patagonian giantess and she had to jump a good foot in the air to get her arms around her twin's neck, Oliver noticed.

James gasped, "You dropped your eggs."

His sister said calmly, "We'll have custard for supper," and kissed him again. Then she dropped Oliver such a graceful curtsy that he found himself sweeping off his hat and making a bow that would have pleased even Master Laneham.

Then Joyce picked up the fowl and the basket. Singularly few eggs seemed to be cracked and it was so well lined with green leaves that it hardly leaked at all.

Everything was well at home, she said in answer to Oliver's question.

"But what's wrong at Campions'?" James asked.

She told them as they walked along. It was almost two

years ago, she said, that it had been discovered that Sir George Desmond, his steward and Father Ambrose were all in one of the Spanish plots against the Queen's life. They had escaped to Spain before they were caught.

"I saw them go," Joyce said. "Isabel was leading Lady Clare up some planks to the ship. She waved to me and called out

that they were going to Ireland. I suppose she thought so. We heard afterwards that they had been seen in Cadiz or Seville—I forget which—and that Father Ambrose and Jonas Oak were both members of the Inquisition. I can't believe it."

"I can," said Oliver. "They tried to find out Drake's plans from me before ever we sailed—and would have if I had known anything to tell—Oak by force, the priest by kindness. But Campions', who owns it now?"

Joyce said that Campions' had been seized by the Crown and was for sale but no one in Boston had money enough to buy it. The manor farm was rented and so were some of the other farms, but the manor house had stood empty ever since the Desmonds left. Trade was bad, she added. The Spaniards had closed ports in the Low Countries and except for fishing boats there were few sails in Boston Harbor. Sometimes coastal ships came, but the port, once second to London, was almost empty now.

"But your father's shop is still busy," she said. "Ever since you took the cittern to the Queen, people have come or have sent to us from all over the country. Some of our viols have even gone to France."

Oliver had been only half listening to her. What he heard was Drake's voice saying, "The meanest, poorest boy of this crew shall have gold enough to be a country gentleman!"

"I'll buy it," he said.

"What?" asked Joyce.

"Why, Campions'," he said—and he did.

James had gone to sea again before they moved to Campions'. He went with John Drake. They had tried to get Oliver to go.

"But he's a farmer at heart," James said disgustedly to John. "He won't even risk half a crown on a voyage. He isn't happy without mud on his boots. He loves pigs. He likes to lean on the pigpen fence and watch them grow fat. He dreams of bacon and hams. What a life!"

It was a life that suited Oliver perfectly. At the end of four years Campions' had begun to look as his mother remembered it from her girlhood. The farms were all rented to good tenants. Flocks of sheep grazed on the broad fields. There were peacocks on the manor house terrace again and the yews were clipped into their proper shapes. There were horses in the stables. Joyce had a white palfrey and Mistress Barrett a brown one. They used to ride to church on Sundays at Boston Stump.

Oliver told Joyce he wished he had found a golden horse with a silver mane for her, but she only laughed and said the white palfrey was perfection. Oliver had no saddle horse of his own. Sometimes he had one of the farm horses rubbed down on Sundays and mounted himself on that. The one the groom brought usually seemed to be too small for him. Perhaps it was chosen on the principle that a short horse is soon curried. He was an amiable hard-working animal, but Oliver looked ridiculous on him, Joyce said, with his feet almost touching the ground.

Why didn't he, she asked, buy himself a Spanish war horse? A black one that pranced? How could he expect any girl to look at him? Why did he never talk to girls about his adventures instead of about the price of wool?

Oliver only smiled good-naturedly and answered none of these questions. He never expected girls to look at him and ask to hear about his adventures. Perhaps Isabel would have. He used to think of her, perhaps in some great palace in Cadiz, dancing the pavane with some handsome haughty Spanish don, but he knew he would never see her again. He had some of his ostrich feathers made into two fans, one for his mother and one for Joyce.

He noticed that plenty of young men looked at Joyce. His mother kept saying that James ought to give her a dowry and then a marriage could be arranged for her. Bostonians of good families did not allow their sons to marry girls without dowries. Mistress Barrett said—and truthfully—that she kept talking to Stephen about it, but that he always said there was plenty of time. So like a man. Oliver should speak to his father.

So one day when he was rowing his father down the River Witham—Stephen Barrett never got on a horse—Oliver said something about a match for Joyce, but Stephen Barrett only smiled and said, "Time enough when James comes home."

James, however, had not come home when the message came to Oliver from Drake.

"Come to Plymouth" was all it said.

He started the day the message came. Joyce could not understand it.

"You mean that you'll leave all you care for, even your precious pigs, and ride off on a horse too small for you just because that man calls you?" Joyce said. "Why does he need you?"

"He'll tell me when I see him, but I know already that the Queen and England must be in danger."

"When will you come home?"

"I don't know."

"Is that how it's always going to be? He'll snap his fingers and you'll come?"

"Yes," Oliver said, "that's how it will be."

"And what of things here—the harvest, the shearing?"

"Things here? Why, Joyce, you'll look after them."

A little more than a week after the message came he was in Plymouth. The groom who brought the horses back to Campions' said that his master had left him at Plymouth Hoe and had said nothing about coming home. Yes, he said, Sir Francis Drake was on the Hoe playing bowls. Finished the game with a real twister, he did.

Oliver had heard at the inn where he stopped that Sir Francis was on the Hoe. He arrived there just in time to see his master bend over to send the bowl across the green turf. The bowl seemed a part of him just as a wet rope he was hauling on seemed part of his arm, just as his feet seemed to grow naturally out of an icy deck. Of course, the bowl followed the path that would win the game for his side.

He made all the proper bows, all the proper courteous remarks to his opponents and to his partners and was soon walking up and down the Hoe telling Oliver the news.

Philip II was collecting a great fleet for an enterprise against England, Drake said. After two years of shutting her eyes and ears, the Queen had at last decided the plans must be checked. On Christmas Eve she had signed Drake's commission for a voyage to the Indies. There had been the usual delays and opposition from the city merchants, but now something had happened that roused even the richest to anger against Spain.

"Have you heard about the *Primrose*?" Drake asked.

Oliver said no and Drake told him the story. There was a shortage of wheat in Spain. There was so little on hand that the bakers had no flour to bake ship's biscuit. It was almost a famine. They sent to England to buy wheat and the safety of an English fleet of grain ships was guaranteed by the Spanish government. One of the ships, the *Primrose*, was quietly unloading her cargo off Bilbao.

"The sheriff of Biscay, Corregidor is their name for him," Drake said, "and a party of his officers, disguised as merchants, came aboard. A pinnace full of soldiers, also disguised, followed. The master of the *Primrose* had warned his crew against treachery. When the Spaniards seized him and called on him to surrender his ship, the crew snatched up their weapons and threw the enemy into the sea. Some swam back to their boats and hurried ashore leaving their friends to drown.

"Our English sailors," Drake went on, "showed more humanity. They fished all the Spaniards they could out of the sea. One of them was the Corregidor himself. They gave him a free passage to London. He had in his pocket King Philip's writ telling him to seize all the English ships and their arms and add them to the fleet he is building to invade England. They had seized plenty of them. Few were so lucky as the *Primrose*. This Spanish courtesy," Drake said, "we will repay and you shall help even the score."

"I hope not as a musician this time," Oliver said smiling. "I did not bring my viols, not even my cittern."

Ever since Drake's message came he had seen himself as an officer of one of Drake's ships.

Drake looked up at him. He saw a strong-looking, tall young man with dark hair curling over his forehead, deep blue eyes and soft black beard.

"No," he said, "not as a musician. As a printer, a Spanish printer." Then seeing Oliver's amazed look, he added, "Yes, I know. You would like to command a ship and it was what I had planned for you but—Do you know Sir Francis Walsingham?"

"The Queen's secretary? Yes, I saw him at Deptford. When the Queen cut your head off—Sir Francis."

"Without Walsingham our heads may all fall, the Queen's among them," Drake said grimly. "Mary Stuart will be on the English throne. Your estate will be seized and given back to Sir George Desmond. King Philip will have his gold again and you, if you are still alive, will be stretched on a rack in the Tower so you will be too busy to come and see me burned at the stake. More than any one man it is Walsingham who has kept us safe. He has agents here at home, in Spain, France, the Low Countries, through whom the news of plots against the Queen reaches him. He needs you."

"For a spy? He cannot know much of me."

"Let us call it an intelligencer," Drake said gently. "He knows of you only what I told him when he asked me for a young man fit for a certain task. I told him I knew a young man who loves the Queen and England. That he has spoken Spanish since he could talk and—because his old nurse came from Cadiz—speaks, no doubt, with the accent of that place. I suppose it has an accent. It all sounds alike to me—like a tree full of parrots talking to a nest of snakes."

Thinking of Drake's Spanish, spoken like English only louder, Oliver smiled.

"Why a printer?" he asked. "Why not a musician or a maker of citterns?"

"For several reasons. Your friends the Desmonds are sometimes in Cadiz, sometimes in Seville and Lisbon where you may also need to go. Even with the beard and your extra height they might know you as a musician. Printer's ink will change you. Moreover, one of Walsingham's best agents is a printer in Cadiz. You will work there, live there. But you must know your trade when you arrive, so that it will not seem strange to his other workmen that he hires you. There is still much to do to equip the fleet before we sail. In one of the print shops here is a man of Walsingham's. He will teach you to read upside down and backwards in Spanish and you'll get printer's ink enough under your fingernails before we sail, I warrant you."

"I can barely read right side up and forwards," Oliver said. "I can see every scale on a fish a gull has caught as well as the gull himself can see the fish before he dives. But when I read, my long arms are barely long enough. I was always far-sighted as a boy, sir, and it grew worse at sea—much worse, sir."

Drake said briskly, "We can cure that easily. Do you remember Zarate's passenger who wore two circles of glass in front of his eyes? They had frames of steel and bows that looped over his ears. He brought them from China and he had others which he courteously left with me. A most convenient toy. I too see better far off, Oliver, than I do close to. I use a pair myself when I look at a chart. The glass is not the same strength in all. I make no doubt there is a pair that will fit you."

Oliver remembered very well how Zarate's passenger looked, rather like a sick owl.

"They will help disguise you," Drake went on. "And we have Spanish clothes large enough for you and black as a night in the Straits. There's a fine warm cloak and even one of those black hats like an old iron bucket and boots of Spanish leather."

Oliver gave up. There was no use in seeing himself on the deck of even the smallest pinnace. His master had evidently thought of everything.

"When do I begin?" he asked.

Drake hit him an approving blow between the shoulders. He had to reach up to do it, but it almost knocked Oliver down on the green turf of Plymouth Hoe.

"Why, now," said Sir Francis Drake, Mayor of Plymouth.

He called a man to him who was standing at the other end of the Hoe, watching the gulls sweep and soar and plunge over the green water or stand like wooden gulls along the sea wall. The man, an agent of Walsingham's as Oliver soon learned, came quickly across the bowling green.

"Master Eaton," Drake said, "this is Master Oliver Barrett who has a fancy to learn the printer's trade. It may be that you can help him."

Master Eaton, a round brown little man, bowed and they set off.

"I will show you the town," he said. "We must not go too hurriedly. We may be watched."

"Who could be watching?" Oliver asked. "Gulls?"

Master Eaton said seriously, "One never knows. One must observe. Do not, if you please, take such long strides. I have to run to keep up. That does not look well. We must stroll."

They strolled. They saw the shipyards. They ate meat turn-overs at a baker's shop and thick slices of freshly baked bread with Devonshire cream and strawberry preserves heaped on them. They saw the new waterworks. They listened to some wandering musicians who played very badly, Oliver thought, but he dropped some pennies into the hat when it was passed to him. It was an English hat of Lincoln green with a peacock's feather in it.

I am going to wear a black Spanish hat like a bucket, he thought gloomily.

Of course, if he saw Isabel she must not know him, but it would be pleasanter if she might think: Who is that tall stranger?—not handsome exactly, but a fine figure of a man. I wonder where he comes from with that soft curling beard. Italy perhaps... Instead, if she looked at him at all, she would see a sick owl—no, a sick raven—no, just a Spanish printer with inky hands and foolish circles of glass balanced on his nose and ears. Never a captain on the deck of his own galleon, or even a pinnace.

Oliver was enjoying feeling sorry for himself. Soon he felt even sorrier.

"Observe the barber's pole," said Master Eaton.

That was a favorite word of his. Oliver obligingly observed it, but could not see that its scarlet and white stripes were different from those of any other barber's pole.

"Go in and have your hair and beard trimmed. You know how Spanish beards look, short and sparse as if they found great difficulty to grow at all. That curly bush of yours belongs on the chin of an English sailor. Have at least half swept up off the floor. Those curls on your head must be subdued. And the mustache, it must droop. Then it will look more melancholy."

"That ought to be easy," Oliver said.

He looked glum enough when he came out. The barber had just let him see himself in a small looking glass.

"We'll soon have you so your own mother will not know you," Mr. Eaton said approvingly.

"Why would she wish to?" Oliver asked.

He smiled because, after all, it was a game and he was beginning to enjoy it.

"You were doing well till you smiled," said Master Eaton. "Scowl any time you feel like smiling and think of drinking vinegar. Now, in this box are several pairs of spectacles. I got them from Sir Francis while you were being shorn. Meet me in my room over the print shop when the clock strikes four. Go down this alley, turn right, then left. Be sure no one observes you. Begin to form the habit now. We will try the spectacles then, give you four eyes instead of two. I will go left here, you go right. Remember—observe, do not be observed."

By the time the English fleet sailed in September, Master Eaton and the printer were pleased with their pupil. He could set type after a fashion. His fingers were suitably inky. He could see to read through the glass circles Master Eaton called spectacles. He could always shove them down on his nose when he wanted to see a ship coming up the harbor. In this way he usually managed to have plenty of ink on his forehead and nose. His Spanish had improved. After the workmen had gone home Oliver would have supper with the printer and they would speak Spanish. The printer came from Cadiz. He had a map of the city and its harbors. He made Oliver study it and tell him how to get from one point to another. He made him shut his eyes and pretend he saw the outer and inner harbors, the shops and churches, the shipyards, gardens, prisons.

It all became as real as Plymouth to Oliver. Indeed, sometimes Plymouth became a dream and Cadiz the place where he lived and breathed. He used to tell the printer and Master Eaton his story and they would question him about it.

Drake, during one of their few meetings on the Hoe, out of anyone's hearing, had outlined the story to him.

"You shall have my name for luck," he said laughing, "and that of the owner of the *Cacafuego*, so you will be Francisco de Anton. You remember Lima? Good. So does Master Eaton. He was a prisoner there. Listen to every word he says about it. You were born in Cadiz. When you were twelve years old, your father took his family to Peru to seek his fortune. He did not make it but died in a mine, buried under falling rock. Your mother died of a fever. You were apprenticed to a printer, but you ran away to sea. You were captured by the infamous corsair Francisco Draque. This is the fate deserved by bad boys who run away from their masters. Draque took you to

England—this accounts for your accent which is, I hear, better than mine, but not perfect. You sailed for Spain with him, but escaped. Master Eaton will tell you more."

He walked on with his rolling gait as if the Hoe were a galleon floating on glassy green waves. Oliver did not see him again until they sailed.

Drake's commission read that he was to rescue the wheat ships seized by Spanish treachery. By the time he sailed, however, most of them had escaped. It was openly said in the fleet that this was a voyage to the Indies. Drake did not even pretend to visit Bilbao. He sailed for Finisterre and then soon came to anchor off Vigo Bay. There, almost under the King of Spain's nose, he stopped to fill his water casks. While his men laughed and marveled at his daring he challenged the governor to choose war or peace. The governor quickly chose peace. They exchanged hostages. One of them, a young journeyman printer, Francisco de Anton, was a prisoner from Lima. He would leave him behind in gratitude for the governor's courtesy, Drake said.

The last Oliver saw of the English fleet, the men were filling casks with storms roaring over them, the ships tossing at their anchors. None of Philip's great Armada, of which all Spaniards were now boasting, came to fight Drake. His ships were soon leaving the bay. Oliver watched them being whirled over a ruffled sea of dark blue and white until the last flapping pennant dipped below the tumbled horizon and vanished.

Chapter 12

CADIZ

The young journeyman printer called Francisco de Anton did not hurry towards Cadiz. Drake had told him to take his time on his long journey south and he did so, earning his living wherever he found work.

"It may be a year—two years—before I return," Drake had said. "You will get news of me through your master. His shop is across the harbor from Cadiz. His name is Juan Enríquez. No kin of our friend the viceroy! You will take your orders from him. He is one of Walsingham's best men. He is a cripple and seldom leaves his shop. You must be his eyes and ears and hands. Forget you were ever Oliver Barrett."

Master Eaton, who was with them in Drake's cabin, gave Oliver directions how to find the house of Juan Enríquez.

He added, "Yes, you must always be Francisco de Anton. Observe all things. Think in Spanish. Speak it to yourself when you are alone. Remember not to be lazy with the letter *r*. Sometimes you may be called on to speak English since you are known to have been a prisoner there. Do not speak it too well. If you are asked questions about England what will you say? Speak in Spanish."

Oliver replied in Spanish that King Philip's Armada would easily conquer England, that his great towering galleons would make short work of the little English ships and that as soon as Spanish soldiers landed, English Catholics would rise and kill the heretics.

"And what else?" Master Eaton had said.

"The English are angry with the Queen because they fear she will marry a Frenchman. They will rejoice to have Mary Stuart as their Queen."

"You say that as a lesson, not as if you meant it," Master Eaton said. "Better not speak of it at all unless you say it with conviction. Better say that the English are too stupid, too lazy, too fond of beef and beer to care who is on the throne. While they can wrestle and play at bowls and bait bears, nothing else matters. Shrug your shoulders and shake your head as you speak of them. Remember they were not unkind to you—they are just children, greedy and foolish. They dance around maypoles when they ought to be drilling as soldiers. When the Armada brings the Duke of Parma's men across the Channel from the Low Countries, they will make short work of the English soldiers."

Drake said, "Unhappily, there is much truth in that. We must see that the Armada never meets the Duke. I will do my part in the Indies, later nearer home. Do yours in Cadiz, Master Francisco de Anton."

He came at last to Cadiz and saw the two harbors, the outer one where great ships from all over the world lay, the inner one where smaller vessels were unloaded. The print shop of

Juan Enríquez was close to the wall of the outer harbor. Early in the morning trumpets were blown in the shipyards calling the men to work. They called Oliver too in Drake's voice, "Do yours in Cadiz, Master Francisco de Anton."

He had a clean little whitewashed room just big enough to lie down in—diagonally. His pallet was stuffed with dried seaweed so the room always had the smell of the sea in it. He covered himself at night with the Spanish cloak Master Eaton had given him. There was an old chest of oak that held his shirts. The room had a narrow slit of a window through which he could look across to the city. It was almost an island city. Only a slender curved arm joined it to the land. It rose white and shining out of misty water at dawn, floated on a blue lagoon all day and seemed to sink again at sunset.

It was at sunset that Oliver first saw it. The white flat topped houses with their Moorish turrets seemed suddenly carved out of gold, then out of pink coral. The dome of the cathedral was a red-gold curve. The masts of ships were golden. Oliver thought of their cargoes: wedges of gold, gold and jeweled chalices, gold-handled swords, gold caskets full of pearls. Nothing, he thought, would shine so bright as the floating city with the golden water rippling around it. Then the sky changed to smoke and flame. The whole city seemed to burn. Soon the blaze was only smoky mist. The city vanished. Only a few twinkling lights showed where it had been.

He came to know its quiet streets and squares well. It was quieter than even a small English town because no wheels rolled along its streets, no red-faced carters bellowed angrily at each other, cracking whips, no ox-carts creaked in the dust. Rich people rode light-stepping Arab horses. Everyone else walked, many of them bent under heavy burdens.

Oliver's own loads were seldom heavy. The chief business of Juan Enríquez was printing lists of naval supplies for the Marquis of Santa Cruz. Oliver used to carry the printed proofs to the palace and wait in the courtyard till they were returned to him corrected. The Marquis, a great seaman, was in charge of building Philip II's Armada for the enterprise against England.

Printed pamphlets showing the progress of the fleet, its arms, its sails, the number of casks of salt fish on hand, were sent to the King, to the Duke of Parma in the Netherlands, to ambassadors all over Europe. People were beginning to call the fleet the "Invincible Armada". Copies of the Marquis's lists of its supplies sometimes reached England as soon as they did the Duke of Parma.

Oliver started the copies on their journey. He walked many miles with the papers sewn in the lining of his cloak to hand them secretly to the next one in the chain of Walsingham's agents. Just how the pamphlets made the rest of the journey even he did not know, but make it they did and news came back from England by the same route. It was from England—not Spain—that he learned that Drake had held up San Domingo in the West Indies for ransom, but it was from a Spanish seaman off a ship in Cadiz Harbor that he heard about John Drake and James Campion.

This man was boasting in a wine shop that he himself had captured Juan Draque, cousin of the corsair Francisco Draque, and the corsair's page, Diego Campione. This happened near the Straits of Magellan.

"If it had not been for me," the sailor said, slapping his chest, "they would be in the Pacific now robbing and murdering instead of in the galleys where they belong."

"What were they like?" someone asked, and the sailor described his captives so that Oliver had no doubts about its being John Drake and James who had been captured. He did, however, doubt that this small wizened man had captured them singlehanded. He said nothing. The sailor had drunk too much sherry to notice that the inky, bearded young man across the table looked ill and sat without touching his plate of beans and peppers and garlic.

Oliver sent a message through Walsingham's secret chain to ask for news of his friends. When the answer came, months later, it was only a sentence at the end of a long message in code. Decoded it read: "No news of J. Drake, J. Campion."

There was, however, plenty of news about Francisco Draque the corsair. It was well known in Cadiz now that Drake had seized San Domingo on January 1st, 1586, saying that he gratefully accepted it as a New Year's gift from Philip II. The governor was so terrified that he had ransomed it for twenty-five thousand ducats.

There were, of course, stories about murder and torture by the corsair, untrue, Oliver felt sure. There was, however, one story that sounded like Drake. A young man who had been a page in the governor's palace told it to Oliver as they were eating dinner in a cookshop.

On the wall of the staircase in the governor's palace in San Domingo there was painted, the young man said, a great escutcheon. It showed a globe with seas and continents. A ramping horse rested one foot on the globe and trampled the air with the others. The motto underneath said: *Non sufficit orbis.*

"That means," the former page explained to the shabby man with the spectacles who did not look well educated or well traveled, "the world is not enough."

"The corsair," he added, "used to stand under it and point to it and ask what the words meant of any Spaniard who came up the staircase. His officers used to gather round him and ask too. This is uncourteous since it embarrassed our Spaniards to answer."

"That was indeed uncourteous. What would they reply?" Oliver asked and gnawed at the drumstick of a Spanish fowl that had led an active and long life.

"Why, that since our King owned the whole globe, he would have to seek more possessions in the skies."

Oliver began on the other drumstick, which was just as tough as the first. It is hard to smile in such circumstances and after working on it a while he was able to look serious and ask, "And what would the English say then? Surely they would not laugh those braying laughs of theirs?"

"The younger Englishmen," the page said, "not only laughed at the reply. They slapped each other on the back in a manner most undignified. The corsair himself, however, kept a decent countenance, but he has a very loud brazen voice and he could be heard down in the courtyard and up in the great hall saying that his most gracious Queen would force the King of Spain to work hard to keep what he had already—such as San Domingo."

"An unmannerly boast," Oliver said. "I hope he did not carry off much treasure with him."

"Our people hid their plate and money and jewels in wells and in other good hiding places," the page said, "but English sailors have keen noses for such things and they carried off many of them. I myself lost a gold chain with a medal of St Christopher which I hid in a flowerpot. I might have done better to keep it round my neck. They never snatched anything anyone was wearing but when they found my chain in the flowerpot they said, 'See, I told you all the dirt here had gold in it.' Besides they captured many of our best ships and broke up our galleys, freeing not only Christian slaves but Turks as well. Also they took guns. Some say two hundred and forty cannon besides rich silks and merchandise."

Oliver shook his head sadly. "I fear this is a blow to our good King such as he has not had since he was King of Spain," he said, and the page agreed.

Later Oliver heard that Drake had also captured Cartagena,

capital of the Spanish Main and had also held it for ransom. Besides, the treasure fleet did not dare sail while the English were in those waters. King Philip's credit was so much damaged that he could not borrow money to go on equipping the Invincible Armada. Also Parma in the Netherlands could not borrow to pay for food for his hungry army.

Oliver wrote of these things in code and started the messages towards England. Before long he heard the best news yet: Drake had returned safely to Plymouth. He had written to Lord Burghley for new orders and had said to him, "My good lord, there is now a very great gap opened, very little to the liking of the King of Spain."

This was all Drake had said of the voyage at which all Europe marveled.

To the printer Francisco de Anton, Drake sent a message in code: "It will not be long now."

Yet it seemed long to Oliver.

News ceased to come from England. In Spain the building of the Armada went on, though under difficulties. One thing lacking was a supply of well-seasoned staves and hoops for casks. Water, wine, salt fish and meat, biscuit and gunpowder all had to be carried in casks. If the staves were green, they shrank. Then the wet provisions leaked and the dry ones spoiled. The Armada could hardly sail without good barrel staves.

Oliver had grown very weary of being a printer. He was homesick for Campions'. The houses of Cadiz glaring in their spring coats of whitewash no longer looked beautiful to him. He was tired of marble and sand and rocks. He dreamed of Campions', of its green fields with the sheep grazing, of hedges, of roses and hawthorn, of wild duck dropping down into the river, of rowing his father across the harbor to Boston Stump.

He still rowed a boat. He had grown fond of his master, Juan Enríquez, and on Sundays he would row him to the city to hear Mass in the cathedral. If they had not gone they might well have found themselves facing the Inquisition, and Enríquez had good reason to fear it.

He was a quiet man with a bent back, a head too large for his small body. He had bright brown eyes in a pale face and a shy crooked smile. His hands were long-fingered and clever at typesetting, but his left arm was twisted and weak. His right leg was shorter than the left one. It was many months before Oliver had learned from him that he came from Kent, that like Drake and Stephen Barrett he had spent his boyhood on a stranded hulk and knew them both. His name was really John Hendricks.

When Mary Tudor was Queen of England and Philip of Spain was her husband, John Hendricks' parents had been burned at the stake. They were heretics. John's mother was a Protestant refugee from Spain. He himself, being only a boy, had escaped with having his body twisted out of shape on the rack. The rest of his life had been devoted to a quiet relentless war between him and the King of Spain.

Through Drake, Hendricks had been employed by Sir Francis Walsingham. Like Oliver he had spoken Spanish from his earliest years. He had now almost lost his English tongue. He and Oliver never spoke it together where anyone might hear them. Indeed, except for those trips across the bay they rarely talked together at all. It was important that the other workers in the shop should see no special signs of friendship between their master and Francisco de Anton.

On each of those Sundays and on other days when he did errands in Cadiz, Oliver had hoped to see Isabel Desmond, but he never had. Probably she heard Mass in some private chapel, he decided, or more likely, she was not in Cadiz at all.

For months after he heard that James and John Drake were galley slaves, Oliver watched every galley that passed him, thinking that one of its shining oars might be pulled by one of his friends. No doubt, he knew well enough, they were still in the Indies, yet there was always a chance. Galleys were used more in Spain than in the Indies, and Cadiz was a meeting place for ships from all over the world.

There was a saying in the wineshops: "You have a friend in China? Wait for him in Cadiz."

So Oliver watched and waited, but at last he gave up hope.

Then one day he saw Sir George Desmond leaning against the wall of the courtyard of the palace where the Marquis of Santa Cruz lived when he visited Cadiz. Oliver felt his breath come fast, quieted it by saying Master Eaton's words, "Observe, be not observed." He observed that Sir George was thinner and older. He had gray in his beard and he looked shorter, but Oliver knew him at once. His listless way of waiting for his horse had not changed and the figure beside him was familiar—Jonas Oak, pale-eyed, fat-fisted, looking as he had at Campions' except that he was now dressed in black in a style well known in Cadiz.

He must be a familiar of the Inquisition, Oliver thought, and felt a little thread of cold run down his spine.

No doubt, he thought, Oak has a natural talent for using the rack, knows just how much will make a prisoner speak without quite killing him.

He walked past them on his errand.

Naturally Sir George did not look up at a shabby young printer, but went on languidly switching his boots with his whiplash.

Oliver thought, Lucky I'm not a horse, or he might have looked at me.

Oak gave him one of his pale stares, but apparently saw nothing more than a dingy young workman in spectacles and black clothes that were beginning to be a greenish brown from hours of sun and rain. Yet for the first time Oliver knew that someone had looked at him who might see Oliver Barrett behind Francisco de Anton. He was glad he did not have to speak until after the two men had mounted their horses and were riding out of the courtyard. He had drilled himself to think in Spanish, but now he could not remember the simplest Spanish words and found English ones racing through his head.

The secretary to whom he was to deliver the proofs came into the courtyard just as Sir George left it. Oliver had a moment of dizziness, but it passed and he went towards the head of the secretary's horse, lowering his head in a respectful bow, and held the bridle while the secretary dismounted. If he stumbled a little in his speech, the secretary did not notice it. He was a handsomely dressed young cavalier who obviously thought himself too good for dealing with printers. However, he liked to talk about horses, Oliver had observed. He "observed" all he could about people, remembering Master Eaton's teaching. He often asked the secretary about horses and Don Alfonso de Rodríguez often generously gave the printer five minutes' intelligent conversation.

This morning Oliver said, "Your Excellency is riding a beautiful new mare this morning. She steps much more lightly than that of the Portuguese gentleman who passed Your Excellency at the gate."

The secretary laughed and said, "Portuguese! It's clear you

have never been far from Cadiz, Anton. The gentleman's from Ireland."

"I thought he sounded foreign," Oliver said, "and is his horse also from Ireland?"

Don Alfonso laughed again, a high laugh rather like a pony whickering, at this ignorance. He gave the pedigrees of his own mare and of Sir George's stallion for several generations while Oliver listened respectfully.

"It's not likely that the father-in-law of Don Pedro de Bazán would be riding an Irish horse," Don Alfonso said. Then, seeing that the young printer was staring at him stupidly, he added, "Don Pedro is a cousin of His Excellency the Marquis of Santa Cruz. He married the daughter of this Sir George Desmond."

"They live here?" Oliver said. "I hope I shall see this señor Desmondo's horse again, since you have told me his pedigree."

"Only while the Marquis is here for a few days now," the secretary said. "They live with him sometimes in Seville, sometimes in Lisbon; that is why it may be that you thought Sir George was a Portuguese."

"No doubt," Oliver said. "Here are the proofs, Your Excellency." He handed over the long lists of supplies and added, "Shall I stay here while Your Excellency corrects them or come back tomorrow?"

"Tomorrow—tomorrow!" said the secretary.

Oliver made another of his best bows, started to go, then turned back and asked, "Has Your Excellency ever seen a golden horse with a silver mane and tail?"

The secretary laughed. "I believe you dream of horses, Anton! Yes, I have seen a gold and silver horse. Isabellas, we call them, after the Queen whose favorites they were. The one I saw belonged to a princess and cost more than a pint of emeralds from the Indies. You had better dream of something else."

"Thank you, Excellency, but after all, dreams cost nothing," said Francisco de Anton the printer.

CHAPTER 13

GALLEY

IN THE spring of 1587 Juan Enríquez sent Oliver on several journeys. Once he sailed on a Dutch freighter to Lisbon and saw there the great galleons of the Invincible Armada and other ships that would be part of the fleet—galleys, brisk little dispatch boats, the lumbering hulks that the Spanish called *urcas*, which carried supplies. He memorized all that he saw and a list in code went to England.

In April he went to Seville, another important center for equipping the Armada. They boasted there that the fleet would be five hundred sails. Oliver thought that among Lisbon, Seville and Cadiz, it might well be a third of that. At Seville there were tons of wheat being ground into flour, and every baker was busy baking biscuit for the Armada. Barrel staves were being shipped to Lisbon. Beef was being powdered with saltpeter. On the wharves, Oliver thought, was enough rope to reach to England. He said so to Don Alfonso de Rodriquez whom he met outside one of the offices from which supplies were ordered.

Don Alfonso was surprised to see the printer from Cadiz

and said with his whickering laugh, "What are you doing here, Anton? Looking for a golden horse? From Barbary?"

"I am on holiday," Oliver said, "but I have an errand for my master as well. Perhaps Your Excellency can help me. I am looking for a writer of plays. Miguel de Cervantes, his name is. My master would like to print some of his plays. I have some of the names here: *La Gran Turquesa, La Batalla Naval, La Confusa*. My master says they are the best plays he has ever seen."

For the first time Oliver saw Don Alfonso show interest in something besides horses.

"Your master is right," he said. "Come! I am busy as always, Anton, but the busiest people can make time, I always say. We'll go to him now. He is a fine maker of plays and a poet too, but in Spain we like to waste everything. Doubtless Cervantes is sitting in a cold room in this very building writing about sacks of wheat with his left hand. His right was smashed to pieces at the Battle of Lepanto. That's what he writes instead of sonnets—stories about flour sacks, how much flour and how moldy!"

They found Cervantes wrapped in a cloak as old as Oliver's at a desk heaped with papers. He was writing with his left hand, his head resting on the useless right one. The room was cold, the windows were dusty. The writer looked thin, shabby, perhaps even hungry, but he had a smile that seemed to warm the chilly, dingy room.

Don Alfonso said, "Señor Miguel de Cervantes, here is a young man who wants you to tell him all about Barbary. He wants to go there and find a golden horse, an Isabella."

Cervantes said gently, "I know little about golden horses. I can tell you something of what it is like to be a slave in Algiers. It is rather pleasant if you have a good master—and I had.

Hassan Pasha was his name. I had plenty to eat, good talk, a good bed. He even gave me paper and ink. I wrote one of my best plays there, *La Confusa*—or was that in jail? I forget. A jail is a fine place to write. You are fed. They had excellent beans in one jail where I was and it was warm in winter. The jailer had a good stove. You can't loiter around the streets and not attend to your writing when you are in jail. You ought to be there yourself, Don Alfonso. Where are the sonnets you were going to show me?"

"Where the tale of your favorite Don Quixote is, señor, in your head and heart," said Don Alfonso. "Like you, I write about ropes and salt fish. Come, put down your pen, señor. We'll dine at a little place I know where they roast pigeons very well. Come too, Anton, and you shall hear a tale about Don Quixote and his horse Rosinante."

Over the roast pigeon señor Cervantes told them a story about Don Quixote spurring his horse, Rosinante, to attack some windmills, which he thought were giants, and being caught by the turning sail and unhorsed. Oliver liked the story; he could not exactly tell why. Perhaps it was the way Cervantes told it—solemnly, but with a twinkle in his deep set eyes.

"You must write it, indeed you must write it, señor," Don Alfonso said, but Cervantes only smiled.

"Oh, for that I must go to jail," he said.

As for the plays that Juan Enríquez wished to print, some of them were printed already, some were lost. Perhaps some day he would find himself in an enchanted castle and write more, but just now he must go back and write about flour sacks.

The next day was Sunday. Oliver was crossing a sunny crowded square on his way to Mass when he heard a familiar sound: Don Alfonso's laugh. Don Alfonso was not a man who would recognize a shabby acquaintance when he was with important people and he was now with his master, the Marquis of Santa Cruz, Admiral of the Ocean Sea. Miguel de Cervantes was crossing the square too. Don Alfonso acknowledged the low bow Cervantes gave him only with a slight lift of his handsome head and such a droop of his heavy eyelids that he did not see Oliver at all.

"No more roast pigeon," murmured Cervantes, smiling as he passed Oliver, who swept off his bucket-shaped hat and bowed because he liked señor Cervantes even if he was not important.

Oliver had seen the Marquis several times in Cadiz and had received orders from him, but the great man never knew him, of course. He looked old and ill, Oliver thought. He was leaning on the arm of a man somewhat younger and rather like him in appearance. With them was a lady in black velvet, short, plump and peevish-looking, and Sir George Desmond.

It was only when he saw Sir George that Oliver realized that the black velvet and pearls and the weary drooping mouth belonged to Isabel Desmond. It must be her husband, Don Pedro de Bazán, on whose arm the Marquis leaned so heavily. Don Pedro, with his gray beard and stringy mustache, looked as old as Sir George. The church was only a short way across the square, but Isabel walked listlessly and as if her feet hurt. Oliver remembered her moving gracefully in the pavane at Kenilworth.

I'm glad James can't see her, he thought. She spoke to her husband in a rattling tone that sounded like her mother's voice, both lazy and shrewish.

Or hear her either, Oliver thought.

He did not see her again. He meant to go back to Cadiz the next day, but he left at once. The Marquis and Don Alfonso went to Lisbon where the Marquis, spurred on by letter after letter from the King, was trying to hurry the fitting out of the Armada. He did his best, but it was not good enough. People said he looked so ill because of the King's displeasure.

Oliver had turned to leave the square before Jonas Oak pushed his way into the group around the Marquis. He did not see Oak, but Oak had seen Oliver. With his spectacles, his height, his very blue eyes and dark hair, his shabby clothes and inky hands, Oliver was not easily forgotten. That he should appear first in Cadiz, then in Seville, made Oak wonder about him. He had seen Oliver bow to Cervantes. Oak left the Marquis and hurried after the writer's thin limping figure. Oak moved quickly in spite of his heavy bulk. Cervantes walked slowly enjoying the sunshine. Oak soon caught up with him.

A heavy hand on Cervantes' lame shoulder jolted him out of his thoughts. To Oak's questions he answered truthfully that he knew nothing of the young man except that he had come from Cadiz and had talked of printing some of his, Cervantes', plays. He could not remember where the printer's master lived, nor his name.

Even if he had known it he might not have told it. Cervantes did not like inquisitors or their assistants, their familiars. Especially their familiars. The inquisitors were sometimes just and honorable men trying to learn the truth, but the familiars were often cruel brutes to start with who became more cruel as time went on. Cruelty is like playing the cittern: it improves with practice. Cervantes did not tell Oak that Don Alfonso had brought the printer to see him but he remembered the inn where they had eaten roast pigeon and he told its name. It was in the opposite direction from the street Oliver had followed.

Oliver had found a small galley just ready to start down the Guadalquivir River, bound for Cadiz, and got passage on it.

The Captain said the galley did not usually carry passengers. It belonged to the Marquis of Santa Cruz, he said, and carried chiefly freight. However—to oblige the gentleman—he accepted a piece of silver and showed Oliver a coil of rope on the bow deck on which he might sit. He went ashore for some food. When he returned to the galley, the last cask had been stowed and the slaves were starting to back her away from the wharf.

Oliver had to jump across a foot of brown water to reach the bow deck. As they swung around and started downstream, he looked back at the wharf. Galloping up to it, swinging off his big horse and running along it faster than he had ever seen so heavy a man run, was Jonas Oak. Oliver could see that Oak was shouting but the Captain at the stern neither heard nor saw him and the boat traveled swiftly down the river.

There were several other passengers whom the Captain had also been willing to oblige, on the bow deck. Oliver did not know if Oak had seen him among them, but that angry shouting face was in his mind all day, except when, instead, he saw Isabel's peevish face and heard her rattling voice. He thought of James too. He had long ago realized that it was foolish to hope to find him. Yet he still hoped.

From where he sat he could see the backs of the rowers. The current of the Guadalquivir carried them on so swiftly that the slaves were not pulling hard at their oars, only keeping their rhythm so that they could turn the galley at any moment at the Captain's orders. Oliver had seen plenty of galleys lying at the docks or speeding across the harbor, but he had never been in one before. This was only a small one, but it had the cruel bronze beak that could shear all the oars off the side of another galley, the shining guns to protect it from being captured, the overseers with their whips walking along on a bench between the chained rowers.

Oliver counted the rowers. There were ten on each side. In larger galleys the rowers were often in darkness below the deck with no light except what came in round the oar holes. At least, Oliver thought, it was better to have light and air even if you were hot or cold, parched or soaked according to the weather. Water evidently splashed into this galley when the sea was rough and rain must fall into it: the men's feet, most of them bare, were in water almost to their ankles.

The Marquis's own galley, in which Oliver had once seen him arrive in Cadiz, was rowed by men in handsome liveries. The men in this one had ragged shirts or none at all. Oliver had seen their faces looking up at him when he had first reached the wharf. He had an impression of eyes glaring out from under tangles of hair stiff with dried sea water. He knew none of them. Now he saw only strong sunburned arms blistered with sun, stained with salt spray and the line of scarred backs bending forwards, then straightening as the oars met the water.

He hated to see the marks of the whip, yet his eyes kept being drawn away from the shining water and the clear skies to the moving backs. What could the men be thinking of as they swayed endlessly backwards and forwards? Were they dreading days of battle or hoping for one as a chance of freedom? Did they think of the homes they had left or were they only wondering whether there would be meat for dinner or only bread and cheese? Or counting the strokes until they would be given sour wine to quench their thirst? And—if Jonas Oak had recognized him—how soon would he learn the answers to these questions?

He found himself beginning to see differences between the rowers. This man's skin was the color of polished bronze and his arms bulged strongly at each stroke. That one's shoulder blades almost cut through his skin. He coughed as he rowed. The sound of the cough was as regular as the clink of fetters and the creak of oars. Another man's bending head seemed too large for his narrow sloping shoulders. Here was one with almost no neck and a bald head. Next to him a long neck supported a small head with an ancient hat on it, a hat of velvet that had once been green with a limp black ostrich feather bobbing at the side. A hole in this man's shirt showed a new whip scar. Blood was spreading on the shirt.

Across the bench, only two oars from the bow, the sun shone on brownish hair with lights of gold in it darker than a bright reddish-gold beard. This man wore no shirt. There were freckles on his back showing between criss-crossed whip scars. There was also a purple scar on his right shoulder like the mark of a claw. Oliver stared at it dizzily.

At last, he thought. Can it be? Yes—No—

So often in the past he had thought he recognized James among the galley slaves he saw—only to realize that his imagination and his hopes had played a trick on him. Still he was always looking, always hoping.

A shout from the overseer made the men on the right of the galley back water while those on the left dug in their oars deeply. The galley spun to the right, avoiding another coming upstream. The Captain recognized a friend. More shouted commands brought both galleys to a stand still. Then both drifted slowly downstream while the captains exchanged ideas about the weather (warm for the time of year) and about the Invincible Armada.

"It will be ready to sail next week—as usual," the captain from downriver said and both laughed.

The men rested on their oars and in each galley turned their faces towards the men in the other. As he saw the long line of profiles turn, Oliver felt no longer dizzy, but both happy and afraid.

Yes! The man with the claw mark on his shoulder was James.

The rest of the passengers—there were only four—had gone to the rail and were looking at the other galley. One of them found a friend who was asking him after the health of his family. Luckily for Oliver there seemed to be at least eleven of them, all with diseases ranging from a slight toothache to a broken leg.

No one noticed as Oliver took one of the dried figs he had been eating and tossed it at the scarred shoulder of the man below him.

James turned and looked up. For the length of time it takes a gull to plunge after a fish, he and Oliver looked at each other. Neither made a sound. Neither even smiled. Many words had never been needed between them. They had often understood each other without speech and they did so now.

Oliver could almost hear James say, "Yes, Oliver, that's you behind those old Chinese spectacles. I know—you want to take the galley singlehanded and free me. You'll drown the overseers and knock out the Captain. What will you use?—that old inkhorn at your belt and your pen case? They'll hit you over the head and the inquisitors will soon have you on the rack. That won't help me or Drake or the Queen. Wait. Think. So will I."

The Captain was saying good-bye to his friend.

"I am your servant. I kiss your hands," he said.

He shouted to the overseers, who cracked their whips and gave the count for the rowers.

"One *two*, one *two*. Put your backs into it, dogs! Dig into it, you lazy pickpockets, thieves, counterfeiters, heretics! One *two*, one *two*. Row, you rascals! Row!"

The passenger with the large unhealthy family said to Oliver, "Are you ill, señor?"

Oliver raised his head from his hands.

"Thank you, señor, I have a slight headache from the glare of the sun on the water. It is nothing."

"Ah, you have my sympathy. My second daughter is troubled in the same way. You should eat plenty of apricots. Nothing is better for the eyes. Eat apricots and you will no longer need those bits of glass in front of your eyes. Perhaps you are a great student and read much by candlelight. Too much reading is bad. You should be more in the open air, as I always tell my third son. He wishes to follow the law. Perhaps the señor too—?"

"No," Oliver said, "I am just a printer."

"If the señor pleases, a little louder? I have a slight deafness, due to a cold."

Oliver was delighted to speak loudly. He said he was a printer, that he worked for Juan Enríquez who did much printing for the Marquis of Santa Cruz, the greatest sailor in the world, who would surely make fish hash with peppers out of the corsair Francisco Draque. The Armada would sail soon, Oliver said. He had just heard the captain say so. He hoped to get a clerk's place with the Marquis and sail on one of the King's great towering galleons—English ships were like floating walnut shells, he'd heard—and be there when the Marquis conquered England. He would show Francisco Draque that he could not seize San Domingo and Cartagena and hold them to ransom unpunished. No doubt the corsair was swaggering around London now, bragging of his robberies and murders, but now that our great King had decided on war, it would not be long now.

The passenger agreed. "Even a little galley like this one," he said, "could do something in battle but if—may I ask the señor's name? A little louder, thank you—if the señor Francisco de Anton had been at Lepanto he would have seen what galleys can do... The señor is quite right; everyone gave credit only to Don John of Austria, but without Bazán—as we old sea dogs call the Marquis—things would have been different."

"The señor commanded a galley under the Marquis, perhaps?" Oliver said politely.

"No, no—only a humble overseer," the man said. "But the galley is a machine. As in a mill or a printing press, the parts must work together. In a great battle even the meanest slave gives something."

He does indeed, Oliver thought. His life, very likely.

He would have liked to throw the talkative passenger overboard, but he went on with the conversation. By the time they reached Cadiz there had been many of these talks and Oliver felt sure he had given James all the information he could need. He had something else to give him too, if he could do it unobserved.

It was wrapped in several thicknesses of linen and sewn into the lining of his cloak. While he was talking, just before they landed, he had found the stitches in the folded cloak and had slowly freed the long narrow bundle. Juan Enríquez had given it to him saying that he would need it if he were ever in prison.

It was a file.

Oliver was the last to leave the deck. He exchanged bows with his deaf friend and insisted on the man's going before him. As he passed James, Oliver stumbled on the bench and dropped his cloak. When he picked it up, the file in its brown linen wrapping was under James's foot in the water.

They did not look at each other but Oliver, as he picked up his cloak, had murmured, "Soon, tonight, if you can. I will watch."

He hurried to the print shop. It was late in the afternoon. Enríquez was not there. He had been rowed to the city to see an important customer, the foreman said. Oliver went to work at once. It was late evening before he had a moment alone with his master. When Enríquez came back, Oliver thought he looked paler than usual, his eyes large, his cheeks more hollow than a week ago. Perhaps he limped no more than before, but he seemed to move with difficulty.

He is hurrying, Oliver thought. He looks ill. Something must have happened.

The time seemed endless till twilight came and the workmen went home. Two pictures kept coming between him and the type he was setting. The first was Jonas Oak's angry face and figure. As he had shaken one of his fat fists at the galley those little gray eyes of his, like small oysters, were half closed and that wide, pale-lipped mouth was a dark hole beneath the purplish-red nose.

If he catches me—Oliver thought—I'll be lucky to be a galley slave... he may be following... he may come soon...

He felt himself stretched on the rack with Oak looking down at him and smiling as he tightened a screw. Oliver shivered and wrenched his mind to the other picture—James's scarred shoulder, his back with the criss-crossed whip marks. Spanish overseers, of course, especially enjoyed beating Englishmen.

But at least, Oliver thought, resetting a line of type he had dropped, "at least he has the file... he has the file... he has the..."

He felt Oak's hand on his shoulder. His legs twisted on the rack. He woke with a start. The shop was empty. The hand on his shoulder belonged to Juan Enríquez, whose eyes were very bright as he said softly, "Drake has sailed!"

CHAPTER 14

SINGED BEARD

"Yes," Juan Enríquez said, "he sailed from Plymouth on April 1st with more than thirty ships. He is bound for Lisbon or Cadiz, more probably Cadiz."

The room which, to Oliver, had been swinging like a turning galley came suddenly to rest. He jumped to his feet saying, "This is the eighteenth. Why, he might be here tonight!"

"Yes, and you must meet him. Row down to the harbor entrance. Take him these charts. I have marked the channels in both harbors. Also the shipyard, where ships lie at anchor, all else I can think of that will help him."

"You must come with me," Oliver said.

"No, I must stay here in the shop till the Armada sails and send him news of it. Then make my way to England as best I can."

Oliver said, "You'll never see England again if you stay. You'll be on the rack or burned. Jonas Oak saw me. He may be following me and that will lead him to you."

He told Enríquez rapidly what had happened in Seville and of finding James in the galley.

"We must wait till dark," he added. "James may come. We'll all go together."

"Very well," Enríquez said quietly. "I will go and meet Drake. He will decide whether I am to return here."

He quickly wrote a letter to the foreman saying that he had been called to Seville on business. He told him to set type for the new lists he had brought that afternoon and to deliver them to Don Alfonso de Rodríguez as soon as possible. He would be gone several days, he said, and he had taken Anton with him.

"The key," he wrote in a postscript, "is in the usual place."

They took only what money they had, a little food, a clean shirt apiece. It was already dark as they finished packing.

"We must leave things looking as if we meant to come back. No, you must not take your books. We'll find others," Enríquez said.

Oliver groaned. "Print them, I suppose!"

"If necessary," Enríquez said.

He blew out the candle. They hid the key under a loose stone, tucked the letter into a crack in the door and went down to the wharf. Oliver helped Enríquez into the boat. The night was growing cool. He put his old cloak over the printer's knees and then went back to the locker for the oars and the rudder.

As he reached the boat with them, he said, "All that troubles me now is leaving James. Shall we wait a little longer?"

A voice in the darkness said, "There is no need, Master Francisco Oliver Barrett de Anton, of here and there and everywhere, printer, circumnavigator, farmer," and Oliver felt himself lifted off the ground by strong wet arms that almost cracked his ribs.

He gasped, "James! How did you do it?"

James said calmly, "Fetch another pair of oars. I am a fairly good oarsman. I'll tell you as we go."

Oliver, with the oars over his shoulder, was getting into the boat when he heard horses traveling fast on the road to the print shop. The creak of leather and the thud of hoofs came clearly across the calm water.

Enríquez said softly, "Shove off and let her drift. They must not hear oars. When they start battering at the door, row as hard as you can."

They pushed off, shipped oars quietly as the trampling hoofs came nearer. The horses had been galloping. Now they were slowing down. As they came near the print shop one of the horses panted so hard that they could hear the gasps above the jingle of bits and spurs and stirrups. In the silence on the water their own breathing sounded as loud as the panting horse and Oliver could hear his blood beating hard in his ears.

Then came the thump of a mailed fist against the door and Oak's voice shouting, "Open in the King's name. Open in the name of the Sacred and Holy Inquisition. John Hendricks, Oliver Barrett, heretics, traitors, English spies."

"Now row," murmured John Hendricks.

Above the sound of their oars they could still hear the battering on the door. Then it ceased suddenly... Torches were lighted.

The printer said, "They are reading my letter. Row a little faster."

As they did so they heard the door crash open. They could see torches shining through the print shop windows. Oliver could still hear Oak's voice across the water.

"What does he say?" John Hendricks asked.

"He says, 'Burn the rats!'" Oliver answered.

"Just as well," the printer said calmly, "in case we left anything he might like to read."

From far down the harbor they could see the print shop burning. At last there was only a faint smoky glow.

"Will they chase us in the galleys?" Oliver asked his master.

"Not yet, I think," said Hendricks. "In my letter I said that we hoped to get passage for Seville in one of the Marquis's galleys. I hope they will hunt for us first where the galleys lie in the inner harbor."

James chuckled, "There's one of old Bazán's galleys they won't find," he said.

"Tell us, James," said Oliver.

"One thing at a time," James replied. "I am not used to talking while I row. And you—heretic, thief, pickpocket,—put your back into it!"

They both put their backs into it and by the time the sun rose they had left the harbor and were lying on the beach of a quiet cove. The boat was pulled up and hidden as well as it could be among the scrubby bushes that grew there.

John Hendricks and Oliver listened while James told the story of the years since he and John Drake had left England to seek their fortune, of their capture by the Spaniards before they ever saw the Pacific, of starvation in dark prisons, of James's sailing at last for Spain, fettered in the hold of a treasure ship.

James did not know what had happened to John, nor did they ever know. When James last saw him, John was answering questions—with the rack where he could see it—about Drake's voyage in the Pacific and an inquisitor was busily writing down what he said.

"Neither of us, I think," James said, "told them anything they did not already know. The passage round the southern most cape is still a secret.

"When we reached Spain and I found myself rowing in the

Marquis's galley, it was a pleasant change," he added. "There was sunshine and fresh air and they did not starve us. That would not be good business. A horse has to have oats and hay. A galley slave gets his bread and onions every day, sometimes even a piece of meat or an apricot. He has plenty of red wine, sour and much like vinegar to drink. The overseer's whip? Why, after the skin is well toughened, you hardly feel it. I mind horseflies more—and fleas."

He broke off a piece of bread and spread it thickly with marmalade made from Seville oranges. After a happy pause he added, "However, I was much pleased when I felt that file under my foot."

"Strange that you and Oliver met as you did," John Hendricks said.

"Stranger still, perhaps, that we did not meet before, using the same harbor, the same docks for a year," said James.

He had waited until the overseer was asleep, he went on. The Captain, the other overseer and the sailors who worked the sails had all gone ashore. The rowers, tired from the long day's work, slept on their benches, their heads bent on their oars.

"Sometimes," James said, "they marched us ashore and chained us up in a dormitory where we had pallets about as hard as the boards under them to lie on. This morning we were to start at dawn so they left us where we were. I liked the galley best—the air is better. When I heard the overseer snoring, I began to file my chain. That was a good strong file. It did not take long. Then I woke my mate and we filed his chain too. He was a Turk captured at Lepanto, has no great love of Christians. He had a few rags of a shirt on his back. We made a gag of that and crept aft. I found a coil of rope and carried it with me. How good it felt to move without a chain clanking between my leg irons!

"We had none on our arms. Our Captain had the opinion we rowed better without them so we were chained only to rings in the floor. Some galley slaves are chained to their oars but our Captain had modern ideas—or had till last night. I don't know what he thinks this morning."

Here James paused and ate a large amount of marmalade with a small amount of bread under it.

"I fear," he went on, "that I hit our overseer rather hard on the jaw. He stopped snoring and we had the gag in his mouth and his feet and hands bound before he even opened his eyes. I cut the rope with his own knife and found the key to the slaves' fetters in his pocket. The Turk bound him to the mast while I was freeing the men. I soon had irons for his feet and for his hands too—that fitted him, not perfectly perhaps, but well enough.

"A strange thing was that the men hardly spoke. We had stuffed our overseer's ears and blindfolded him when we gagged him. There was little for him to hear. It was as if all had been planned and each knew his part. The Turk went among them saying to them softly, 'Africa?' All nodded and grasped their oars. There was one man—another Turk—who wished to kill the overseer but my friend said, 'No, let us not act like Christians,' and the men started rowing all together as if they were chained.

"When we came near your wharf—I had often seen the big rock with the old oak growing out of it that you told the passenger about, Oliver—I embraced my Turk, waved good-bye to the others and dived into the water. I pulled myself up on the wharf just as you went for the oars."

He yawned and asked, "Shall we take turns watching and sleeping now? The night was long."

Oliver was on watch that afternoon. It was hard work to keep his eyes open. There was a fresh breeze from the south-west that made the hot sun dance on the blue water and dazzle his eyes. Clouds rising in the west were like the sails of ships hull down on the horizon. He felt his eyelids close as he watched them. John Hendricks had brought his hour glass in his bundle. He had set it on a salty piece of gray driftwood. The red sand was running fast through it now. It would soon be four o'clock and time to wake James from his sleep.

James was sleeping as peacefully as he might in his own bed. His beard and the darkening of his hair in the last years had changed him, of course, but there was something about the half smile on his lips, the way the hair fell over his freckled forehead, the outline of his short straight nose that could be only James.

John Hendricks stirred often in his sleep. Sometimes his lips moved. Once he opened his eyes wide and looked at Oliver without seeing him, muttering, "the rack—the rack!"

Oliver shivered in the hot sun, thinking: He would be on it now, but he would not speak. That I know.

He looked down at the printer's twisted body and thought: He has patience, courage, fortitude. As much as James, as much as Drake. I think he is the bravest man I know.

The last grains of sand fell. Four o'clock.

Oliver looked again at the clouds that were like sails and they were sails.

He stared at them for a moment. He knew what their names must be. John Hendricks had told him there would be four

Queen's ships, strong swift galleons: the *Elizabeth Bonaventure*, the *Dreadnaught*, the *Rainbow*, the *Golden Lion*. There they were, with the sun on their sails, little more than a mile away.

He shook James out of his sleep. Hendricks woke too and heard him say, "He's here, James! Drake's here! There's the *Elizabeth Bonaventure*!"

Hendricks said, "Quick with the boat. We must reach him with the charts before he enters the harbor."

It was hard rowing against the wind, but James enjoyed himself by making sounds like the crack of a whip.

"Come on, heretic," he shouted. "Crack! No sleeping at the oar! Crack! What would our good King Philip think? Crack!"

Their good King Philip was in his garden enjoying his flowers. For once he was taking an afternoon away from his desk. On it was a great pile of dispatches he had not read. One of them had come by courier from his ambassador in France, through rain and mud and scorching sun and dust, as fast as a man can ride. The message said that Drake had sailed from Plymouth on April 1st, probably to strike Cadiz.

No one in Cadiz that afternoon had heard the news. A company of strolling players was in town and the more fashionable citizens were watching them act a comedy. Others were enjoying the antics of a tumbler who was showing his skill in the great square. No one hurried to look when the news came that a fleet was heading towards the harbor. There were already ships from Spain, Italy, Portugal, France, Holland and Denmark in the outer harbor and sailors from them in the wineshops. Why not others? Ships from the Levant, perhaps, or from Biscay or from the East Indies loaded with spices and silk? Porcelain and ivory from India, gold from Peru, ostrich feathers from Patagonia—ships brought them all to Cadiz. So why not this afternoon? And why hurry to look at them?

Drake, however, was in a hurry, too much in a hurry to be surprised by having charts brought to him in a small boat by three men he had not seen for years. His blue eyes took in the marks on the chart with their usual speed. His ears heard and understood all Hendricks had to tell him. He thanked them, turned them over to one of his pages to see them fed and clothed, raised a signal that called his captains to council.

Oliver, washed and dressed in English blue cloth, with his spectacles in his pocket, felt like an Englishman again. Drake called him and James and John Hendricks to join him on the quarterdeck where he was discussing plans with his captains. Some advised Drake to wait outside the harbor and attack in the morning. William Borough, captain of the *Golden Lion* and vice-admiral of the fleet, thought they ought not to stay too long outside. He said they could hold a council, make plans, give orders and—if the wind held—get into the outer harbor by eight o'clock.

"We shall not stay at all," Drake said and sailed on towards the harbor entrance, leaving the other captains to get back to their ships and follow as fast as they could.

Galleys tried to stop him from entering the outer harbor. They made a fine show, as James said, if you had never been a galley slave. These were large galleys such as fought at Lepanto, he told Oliver, and their rowers probably had shirts. The King's flag billowed from their mastheads and their bronze beaks were ready to pierce the sides of the English ships. Their bow decks were crowded with soldiers ready to board the enemy as soon as the shining oars brought them alongside.

They came close enough so that Oliver could hear the

cracking of the overseers' whips. Then the English trumpets sounded. The Queen's flags were run up to the mastheads and English cannon balls began to crash round the galleys. Their commander did the best he could to delay Drake's ships from reaching the city, but he was no match for the Queen's galleons.

Oliver saw a young page—could he ever have looked as young as that?—jumping up and down squealing, "See! The cowards are running away!"

Drake heard him and said, "Not cowards at all. Their commander knows his work. Galleys are to fight galleys, not ships of war. Waste no more powder on them," he said to the master gunner. "Save it for the ships."

The ships gave them little opposition. There were, according to Oliver's count, at least eighty of them: freighters loaded with wine and biscuit for the Armada at Lisbon, ships from the Mediterranean bound for France, others on their way to the West Indies, Sweden, Italy. There were even a few Spanish ships bound for England, loading on casks of the wine of Xeres, which the English call sherry.

Only one of all these ships was ready to fight. Those that could make sail hurried to escape. Some made for the upper harbor, others for shallow water. Most of them could not even raise their sails, since their crews were ashore, but swung helplessly at anchor. The one that fought was from the Levant and loaded with cochineal and wool for Italy. Her captain had cannon and powder and shot and the courage to use them, but English guns had a longer range and were better aimed. She was riddled with shot and sunk.

Drake anchored among the rest of the ships, took what prizes and cargo he needed, burned others. By eight o'clock, the time Vice-Admiral Borough had suggested entering the harbor, it was already ablaze and looked as it had when Oliver first saw it with walls and turrets pink in a smoky glow.

By dawn the work in the outer harbor was finished. There was still a task to be done in the inner bay. James had told Drake that close to the entrance lay a galleon belonging to Old Bazán, as James and his other galley slaves called the Marquis of Santa Cruz.

"The talk on the galley, sir, is that she will be the flagship of the Armada—the Invincible Armada, sir. Yesterday she was taking on stores and there are soldiers ready to sail in her," he told his master.

James and Oliver, armed with arquebuses, went with Drake in his barge. His pinnaces and the *Merchant Royal* from London followed him. They burned Old Bazán's galleon and some of the smaller ships that had escaped into the inner harbor the night before.

By noon Drake was ready to leave, but the breeze had dropped. For twelve hours there was not a breath of wind. The English ships with useless sails and drooping flags and streamers swayed idly on the glaring green water. Shore guns and galleys attacked them but did little damage. Towards night the Spaniards sent fire ships against them and again Cadiz was pink in the flaming glow.

Even the fire ships were useless against the English ships. As often as they came near, pinnaces met them and towed them off into shallow water where they burned.

Drake called out so it was heard on one of the pinnaces, "The Spaniards are doing our work for us, burning their own ships."

This jest had soon echoed through the fleet. Sailors bawled from one top mast to the next, "Hey there, mate—did you hear

what the Admiral said? He says the Spaniards are doing our work for us. Burning their own ships. Ho, ho!"

By midnight the fires had died down. A little air stirred, enough for Drake's fleet to move through the Channel. The galleys followed him. At dawn he anchored and challenged them to fight him. The Spanish commander had seen enough English broadsides. He declined the invitation politely and sent Drake some excellent sherry, orange marmalade, sugared chestnuts and a suggestion that they should exchange prisoners.

There were Englishmen in the galleys who found themselves on English ships again. Some of them had almost forgotten their English speech. Oliver had to translate into Spanish for one of them what Drake said as the fleet set sail.

"Well, my friends," he called. "We have singed the King of Spain's beard."

As this saying too was shouted through the fleet, the former prisoner said in Spanish, "But it will grow!"

"He knows that," Oliver said.

CHAPTER 15

A GAME OF BOWLS

D RAKE KNEW that his work was only begun. He wrote to Walsingham, "I dare not almost write of the great forces we hear the King of Spain hath. Prepare in England and most by sea! Look well to the coast of Sussex!"

He himself looked well to the coast of Portugal. The Marquis of Santa Cruz was at Lisbon waiting for supplies, powder and shot, for biscuit and barrel staves. He needed sailors and soldiers too. For weeks men and supplies did not reach him because the English fleet was between him and Cadiz. Drake had captured the castle at Sagres on Cape St Vincent. He cruised off the Cape for several weeks. Ships from the Mediterranean, bound for Lisbon, carrying soldiers and provisions for the Armada, went no further than Cadiz.

Drake seized no prizes that seemed important, but there were many of them, mostly fishing vessels and small freighters; many of the freighters were carrying hoops and staves. By burning and sinking these ships, Drake knew he was dealing the Armada a worse blow than when he burned Old Bazán's flagship. For the Spaniards had to use casks of unseasoned wood (since Drake had destroyed the seasoned staves). These casks leaked, supplies were lost and the Armada suffered—mainly from shortage of water.

By the middle of June when Drake's fleet left Cape St Vincent, he wrote to Walsingham saying, "We have, although it be little, made a beginning."

Before he sailed for England he heard of the *San Felipe*, a carrack from India, bound for Lisbon. He knew that she was full of spices. Perhaps she might carry gold and jewels. Queen Elizabeth's navy was supposed to pay for itself at sea. Here was a rich prize worth all the ships in Cadiz Harbor. Drake determined to seize her, and seize her he did. He was right about her value. Her silk, ivory, cinnamon, gold and rubies were worth more than a hundred thousand pounds.

Drake was not the only Englishman who knew that what he had done was only a beginning. Important men like Walsingham and John Hawkins knew it. So did the sailors who laughed when the King's beard was singed. So did John Hendricks and James Campion and Oliver Barrett.

Hendricks went off on another mission, to the Netherlands this time. James was given command of one of Drake's pinnaces. He named her the *Isabel*. Oliver had asked permission to give up the sea and go back to Campions'.

"Not till we have finished what we have begun," Drake said. "Go and stay a week, but come back to Plymouth."

So James sailed into Boston Harbor with Oliver as a passenger and for a week there was rejoicing at Campions'.

It was all as Oliver had dreamed of it in Cadiz. There was the cool green shade, and the hedges full of roses, the gulls sailing and swooping around Boston Stump, the peacocks spreading their tails among the clipped yews. They screamed by day and nightingales sang at night, just as he remembered. The sky was softly blue with great billows of drifting clouds, not the hot clear blue skies of Spain. The strawberries tasted like English strawberries.

Only one thing was lacking. Joyce was not there. She had gone to visit cousins at Tweedmouth, which was far in the north, almost as far as Scotland, and would not be back for weeks.

They hoped, Oliver's mother said, that a marriage might be made for her there. Her cousins knew a leather merchant, they said. It was hard to arrange a marriage for a girl with no fortune. Of course, if James had other ideas—or if Oliver did?

James had the idea that Joyce ought to stay at home and attend to the dairy. Galley slaves did not come home with gold in their pockets, he said, and why should he give his sister to some fat leather merchant? And he would like some more strawberries.

Oliver was no more helpful. He could not believe, he said, that Joyce would like to leave Campions' and she would always have a home there. Of course, if she found someone she liked, he and James would manage something for her, no matter what James said. Trade would improve after Drake had beaten the Armada. The wool shining on those sheep two fields away would be worth something then. And how was his father's business?

"Ever since you took the cittern to the Queen, it's not been bad," Stephen Barrett said, so Oliver knew it must be very good.

James said suddenly, "I wonder where Isabel is dancing now?"

Oliver had not told him that Isabel was now a fat peevish Spanish señora with a husband old enough to be her father and he did not say so now. It seemed cruel to do so. Besides, it was all part of his story as Walsingham's agent, and in the hall at

Campions', with the workmen waiting till supper was over to make music, he did not speak of it. His parents knew nothing of his life as a printer or of Jonas Oak or of John Hendricks. These things were for Secretary Walsingham's ears, not theirs.

The ink was out of Oliver's fingernails now. There was no trace of the wandering Spanish printer and his bucket shaped hat, though he still had a shabby old cloak and the spectacles he used while reading.

He thought that sometime after Drake had beaten the Armada, he and Joyce might be sitting in the rose garden and he might tell her about it.

I wish the Armada would come soon, he thought.

Of course he knew as he sailed back to Plymouth and waited there that it could not come soon. The Cadiz raid and what they had done at Cape St Vincent had delayed it, as Drake meant to do, yet he and all his men wished it would sail.

When spring came in 1588 it was at last certain that the Armada would sail—and soon. Walsingham received reports, one of them from John Hendricks in Brussels, that the Duke of Parma's well-drilled army would be met by the great fleet and transported across the Channel. The landing point was already decided on. It would be near Margate. As soon as Parma's troops landed, English Catholics would rise all over the country and kill Protestants. They would kill the Queen, and England would become a Spanish province.

These were not secrets that Hendricks had difficulty in finding out, he said. The Spanish plans were common talk everywhere.

Now beacons were set up and down the land. When they began to flame, the news would travel swiftly all over the country that the Spanish attack was at hand. Bells would sound. The trained bands would muster on village greens. Forts along the coast would shoot their cannon. King Philip's soldiers would receive a royal welcome on land.

For the sea John Hawkins had been making ready such a fleet as had never been seen. The new English ships were long, low, and narrow, and decked over at the waist. They carried longer-ranged cannon than the Spanish ships. They could sail faster and closer to the wind than ships had ever sailed before.

Older ships were rebuilt on the lines of the new ones. All that winter English galleons were being careened, scraped clean of weeds and rubbed with tallow. Guns were being cast, cannon balls heaped up, sails and cordage made ready. The English captains called their ships the best in the world. Drake was not alone in wishing to try his ships against the Spanish galleons.

Yet no Spanish ships came that spring. King Philip had ordered the Marquis of Santa Cruz to get the Armada to sea by February 15th at the latest. The Marquis had tried his best, but he never sailed against England. He died on February 9th, some said of a broken heart because of the reproaches he received from the King.

Philip now appointed the Duke of Medina Sidonia to be his Captain General of the Ocean Sea. Like Lord Howard of Effingham, the Duke was chosen because he belonged to a great and noble family rather than because he was an experienced seaman. The Duke wrote to the King's secretary that he had no experience of the sea or of war.

"I am always sick at sea and always catch cold," he wrote.

He added that he did not feel able to command so important an enterprise. Philip, however, had made up his mind and he did not change it. The Duke of Medina Sidonia became the commander of the Invincible Armada.

No one in England thought that the coming battle would be between two great noblemen, the Duke of Medina Sidonia and Lord Howard of Effingham. They did not even think of it as a battle between their Queen and the ruler of the greatest empire in the world. Not only in England but in France and Holland, even in Spain, men spoke as if the struggle were between Drake and the King of Spain. In England it was always, "Drake has so many ships... Drake will save us... Drake will sail..."

On the Continent they still called him a pirate but they still spoke of Drake's ships and Drake's guns.

Drake himself would have been the first to laugh at this talk. He knew how hard it had been to get the Queen to allow either ships or guns to be made ready. He knew, better than anyone else, the power of Spain. He did not laugh when he read a copy of the Duke of Medina Sidonia's letter. Even if the Duke caught cold easily and was sick at sea, the battle would not be an easy one, Drake knew. He did not underestimate the enemy. Neither did he fear him. Like his cousin John Hawkins, he was eager for the swift English ships to show what they could do against the Spanish galleons.

He had plenty of information about the Armada. The Duke had a complete account of his preparations printed; very well printed, Oliver thought, as well as Juan Enríquez could have done it. It told the name and tonnage of each of its one hundred and thirty ships—galleons, galleasses, galleys, urcas, fregatas, pataches. It told the names of their captains, the numbers of their soldiers and sailors, the names of gentlemen adventurers, gunners, priests. It listed guns and other arms. There were 123,790 cannon balls besides matches and powder and lead to cast bullets. It told how many casks of biscuit and wine there were.

Oliver brought Drake a copy of the report, which John Hendricks had sent across the Channel.

"Why do they tell all this to the world?" Oliver asked Drake. "Do they not know the news will reach us before their ships can move a foot towards England and that you will make ready for them?"

"They hope to put terror in our hearts," Drake said, "but cannon balls on paper do not make my teeth chatter—much."

Oliver laughed. He thought of Drake in Cadiz Harbor on the *Elizabeth Bonaventure* with real cannon balls crashing and splashing around him, fire ships flaming, galleys thrusting their beaks at him.

"No, I cannot hear them chatter," he said.

The astrologers had foretold awful things about the year 1588. Eclipses of the sun and moon, strange meetings of planets were at hand. The least evil things in store were bad weather, earthquakes, plagues. The worst ranged all the way from war and the destruction of empires to the end of the world. At least the astrologers were right about the weather. When the Armada was ready to sail in May, it met gales like those of December. On the fourth of May, when it left Lisbon, a bitter wind blew right into the mouth of the Tagus and kept the fleet from getting to sea. It anchored and lay there for two weeks.

Drake had plenty of time to study the printed lists of the Armada and its equipment. He learned that in the first line there were two strong squadrons, ten galleons from Portugal—Portugal now belonged to Philip—ten from Spain, with four ships from the West Indies fleet and four galleasses from Italy. A galleass' oars made it possible to move without wind.

The second line had forty-one ships, former merchant men,

heavily armed. For scouting and carrying messages there were thirty-two light swift pataches and fregatas. There were twenty-five big urcas to carry supplies and four galleys like those in Cadiz Harbor.

"How many does that make, Oliver?" Drake asked.

"One hundred and thirty in all, sir," Oliver said. "They talked of five hundred when I was in Spain."

"That would have needed even more barrel staves," Drake said. "I'll warrant by now their casks are leaking."

Then for weeks they knew little more about the Armada than the pamphlet told them. There were rumors that the fleet had sailed and had been battered to pieces by great storms. The storms were real enough, but they had not sunk the Armada. At last they heard on good authority that it had indeed been damaged and that many ships had been blown far away from the main body of the fleet. However, most of them had rejoined the Duke's flagship, the *San Martín*, and they would soon sail.

Lord Howard, John Hawkins and Drake had all been eager to attack the Spaniards on their own coast but the Queen had never given her permission. At last she sent word that her fleet might sail for Spain. The wind blew briskly from the northeast. More than ninety well-armed English ships set off to meet the Armada.

They returned to Plymouth without a glimpse of it. The wind veered to the south-west. It would blow the Spaniards to England. Drake knew that if he kept on beating his way against it, the Armada might be attacking English ports long before the Queen's ships reached Spain. On July 12th they anchored again in Plymouth Harbor.

One of the ships that sailed out to meet the Armada and then came home again was the pinnace *Isabel*, commanded by

James Campion. Another was the *Rejoice*, also a swift pinnace. Her captain was Oliver Barrett. No doubt Lord Howard of Effingham was proud of his flagship, the *Ark Royal*.

He wrote to Burghley that she was "the odd ship of the world. We can see no sail, great or small, but how far so ever they be off, we fetch them and speak with them."

Certainly the Duke of Medina Sidonia took pride in the *San Martin* with her great banner with the arms of Spain on it, her painted sails and her towering castles. Yet neither the Lord High Admiral nor the Captain General of the Ocean Sea can have been so happy as Old Bazán's galley slave and his journeyman printer with their first commands. The *Isabel* and the *Rejoice* were as clean as ships could be. Their sides were properly scraped and tallowed. Masts and spars shone like Stephen Barrett's viols. Their cannon winked in the sunshine. The decks were as clean as the floor in the great hall at Campions'. Their sails were like June clouds.

When they reached Plymouth on July 12th, the talk there was that the Spanish fleet was too damaged to sail that summer, that the Queen's galleons would be laid up. Drake went on with his preparations as if he had never heard these rumors. The contrary wind and the delay really helped the English fleet. It had started short of food. The new ships were tight and trim but some of the merchant ships, which had been armed as ships of war, started to leak. There were spars and cordage and blocks to be replaced. All the ships were short of food and of wood and water. During a busy week all these needs were supplied and they took on extra supplies of powder and shot. They would need all they could carry to meet those 123,790 cannon balls of the Duke's.

By July 19th the English fleet was ready for sea again. Its

commanders ate dinner on board their ships. The *Rejoice* was anchored near Drake's ship, the *Revenge*, and Oliver, during his own dinner, could hear music drift across the water. The tunes were the old ones he had often played and that James had sung. One of the young pink-faced pages had a high sweet voice.

> *"Pastime with good company,*
> *I love and shall until I die,"*

he sang.

After he stopped, Drake set out for Plymouth Hoe for a game of bowls. He had asked Oliver to come and be one of his team.

"For an inky-fingered printer, you cast a good bowl, if I remember," he had said.

When Drake's boat started for the Hoe, Oliver's followed it. Others joined them—James's neat little shallop, even Lord Howard's barge with oarsmen handsomely dressed in his livery. Lord Howard did not play, but Oliver heard him making a wager on Drake's side.

As he stood there watching Drake making ready to hurl the jack along the smooth green turf, Oliver thought of the many times he had seen his master's sturdy figure bent for the throw. There had been an evening at Boston, he remembered, with Master Doughty's shadow very long on the grass. In Patagonia there was a hard-packed level strip of sand. The day was bright and cold. Frosty wind nipped fingers. The giants gathered on a hill and watched the strange motions of the small man below them.

In Peru Drake had found a field where the llamas had nibbled the grass so that a bowl could take something like its proper course towards the jack. They had used a sandy beach again in California, and Oliver remembered the Indians murmuring and bowing their heads at the white man's magic as a bowl curved across the sand and knocked another out of position.

The pictures all flashed through Oliver's mind as Drake hurled the jack and it came to rest more than twenty-five yards across the green. It was Oliver's turn and he was just weighing the bowl in his hand when Thomas Fleming came hurrying, almost running, across the green.

Fleming was commander of a bark that had been cruising the mouth of the English Channel watching for the Armada. He had seen it, he gasped out to Lord Howard and Drake, a great fleet of Spanish ships with furled sails lying off the Scilly Isles.

"They are waiting for the rest to come up," he panted.

He was still out of breath from his dash across the Hoe.

There was a moment of silence on the green. Drake broke it by saying cheerfully, "Come, gentlemen! We have time to finish the game and beat the Spaniards too."

The players all knew that Drake was right. Both wind and tide were against them. They would gain no time by trying to get out of Plymouth Sound before the tide turned. They could finish the game.

By the time the Queen's galleons were warped out of the sound to anchor near Rame head, everyone in the fleet had, as usual, heard Drake's new saying.

"Did you hear what he said? Did you hear what Drake said?" had been shouted from ship to ship.

What he said did not always sound the same. It was repeated in the crisp speech of Londoners, in north of England accents, some of them almost Scottish, in the slow soft tones of the West country. Sometimes adjectives not polite to the Spaniards were added. Sometimes, as he spoke, Drake made a wonderful forehand throw that sent the bowl curving to the right on a miraculous path between five other bowls and come to rest just touching the jack. Or he threw backhand and the bias carried the bowl to the left. In another version he delivered the bowl straight with such fierce speed that it knocked the only threatening bowl out of the way. One reporter, more poetic than the others, said that he spoke quietly and that the bowl slid gently to its winning place like a dark pearl on green velvet. No one liked this version much except its inventor. It was generally agreed in the fleet that he swung across the green with his rolling gait and spoke in the tones of a trumpet.

But wherever the story went, whether the speaker called him Frankie or Frank Drake, Sir Francis, the Vice-Admiral, or just Drake, it brought laughter and courage and confidence with it.

Lord Howard, confident too, said, "The southerly wind that brought us back from the coast of Spain brought them out. God blessed us with turning us back."

The game that Philip of Spain had begun would now be played.

CHAPTER 16

THE ARMADA

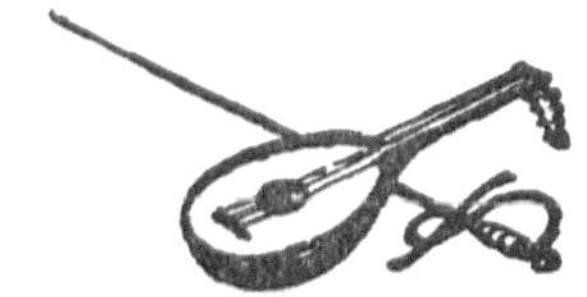

IT WAS not only on Plymouth Hoe that men knew the Armada had come. Soon it was sighted off the Lizard, and beacons began to flash fire carrying the message to all England. From the Queen to the mother of the youngest ship's boy in the fleet, all women knew what the drifting, glowing smoke meant. It called men to every village green from Devonshire to Northumberland. Beacons lighted the white cliffs of Dover, shone on the towers of Kenilworth Castle, sent smoke swirling around Boston Stump. When it was seen, bells began to ring.

Now was the moment English Catholics were supposed to rise against their Queen and start killing their neighbors. The beacons were not only a signal to heretics that the Armada was at hand. They also told Catholics that Parma and his soldiers would soon be crossing the Channel to the mouth of the Thames.

When they landed, England would be a Spanish province. Smoke would keep rising in it but not from beacons—from heretics burning at the stake. Yet as it happened, when the bells woke English Catholics so that they looked out and saw the signal lights, they either turned over in bed or got up and went to help their neighbors fight the Spaniards. They were, after all, Englishmen.

On the afternoon of Saturday, July 20th, Drake sent Oliver on a scouting expedition. James had gone out earlier but had not come back. Oliver sailed out from behind Rame Head where the fleet lay and out past the boiling, roaring Eddystone. He climbed his own mast and looked west. There it was, dark against the western sky, the Armada. It made the sea look as if it had changed suddenly to land. Now it was a sea-coast, edged with a wall of towering castles, how many he could not count. A path of rippled gold led to a great crescent, a dark forest of masts, to clouds of painted sails, the Invincible Armada.

Dazzled by the glare, Oliver tried again to count the ships but suddenly rain clouds covered the sun. Mist and darkness rose from the sea. He dropped to the deck, sailed back to Rame Head. As he reached it, Oliver saw the *Isabel* just anchoring. He anchored beside her and he and James rowed the *Isabel's* boat to the *Revenge* to make their report to Drake.

James had not been content with trying to estimate the size of the Armada from a distance. He had sailed among them and

had replied to their fire with his own cannon, the first shots exchanged by the Armada and an English ship.

"Of course," James said, "my guns are only popguns, but I thought it was only courteous to reply. My shots did no harm. Now if I only had a galleon—"

"If you had a galleon you would be where galleons belong," Drake said, "obeying the Lord Admiral's commands. And did he or even his vice-admiral order you to defeat the Armada single-handed?"

"No," James admitted, "but you told me to look well at it. I did."

James's impertinent challenge to the Duke of Medina Sidonia was too much like some of Drake's own exploits to earn James much of a reprimand.

Drake merely said rather dryly, "You may report what you saw, Captain Campion."

"I knew some of the ships," James said. "There were big Levanters such as I've seen in Cadiz, and galleasses in the van. Then came the Duke's galleons. I counted twenty but there may be more. I saw no galleys. The poor slaves may have been drowned in the storms. The urcas were in the center and there were galleons from Biscay in the rear and I saw ships from

Portugal. I counted over a hundred ships and missed many, I think. They have more than we but I like our ships better. More nimble. Now if we can just get to windward of them—"

On Sunday morning the English fleet was to windward of the Armada. It was a great feat of seamanship to leave a lee shore, slip round the Spanish fleet and get the weather gauge. Eleven English ships were still to leeward when the Spaniards first saw them, but they sailed clear of the Levanters in the van and stood off on a new tack to join what both Spaniards and Englishmen called Drake's fleet.

Drake himself always treated Lord Howard with great courtesy. Still he probably thought of the fleet as his too. Even Lord Howard may have thought of it as Drake's fleet but his report of that day's work says only that "the next morning, being Sunday, all the English were come out of Plymouth and recovered the wind of the Spaniards two leagues to the westward of the Eddystone."

No doubt the Spaniards were amazed at the way the English ships could use the wind, any wind it seemed, for their purpose. The towering galleons could not shift from one tack to another with any such speed, nor fly so fast before it. However, the amazement was not all on one side. When the *San Martin*, the Duke's flagship, saw the English ships to windward, the Duke ordered a signal gun fired to show he expected an English attack. His fleet at once formed in battle order. Before the eyes of the astonished English sailors, the whole Armada formed into a great crescent that moved forwards along the Channel more like an army than a fleet. The tips of the crescent were almost seven miles apart and pointed towards the enemy. Some of the best-armed galleons were at the crescent points to protect the urcas, which sailed in the thickened center of the quarter-moon.

Drake saw at once the great strength of the formation. If he kept the weather gauge, he could attack only the biggest and best-armed galleons on the points of the crescent. If he damaged one, it could retreat into the center and another would take its place. If an English ship got between the crescent points, its speed would be worth nothing. The crescent would close like the jaws of a great dragon. The teeth of the dragon, those threatening castles, would seize it and grind it to pieces.

On Sunday, July 21st, the Duke of Medina Sidonia hung out his sacred banner to show he was ready for battle. Lord Howard answered his challenge by sending a bark, the *Disdain*, to say that he was ready. Then Lord Howard in the *Ark Royal* formed his ships in line and sailed against the northern tip of the crescent. He exchanged shots with the Levanters without giving or receiving much damage.

At the same time Drake in the *Revenge*, Hawkins in the *Victory* and Frobisher in the *Triumph* attacked the other point of the crescent. There they found one of the most skillful of the Spaniards, Vice-Admiral Juan Martínez de Recalde. He tried to bring his ship, the *San Juan*, close to the English ships. He knew that victory lay in grappling and boarding them, but he could not come close enough to hit them with his short-range cannon. They stayed three hundred yards away and shot cannon balls at him until he was damaged and retired to the center for repairs. Another big galleon took his place.

The Duke himself tried to close in on Drake's squadron but the swift English ships only slipped away to windward. If the Spaniards came too close, cannon balls splashed round them and the enemy was as far away as ever. The only ship injured that day was the *San Juan*. Though she had some killed and wounded, most of the damage was a matter of spars and stays to replace.

Neither Lord Howard nor Drake was proud of that day's fight. Howard wrote to Walsingham for more ships and men and said he dared not venture among the Armada. It was too strong.

Drake wrote, "We had them in chase and there hath passed some cannon shot between some of our fleet and some of them and as far as we perceive, they are determined to sell their lives with blows."

The only serious losses the Spaniards had that day were accidents that took place after the day's fighting was over. One ship collided with another and lost its bowsprit. On another gunpowder exploded, killing many of the crew. The ship was saved from complete destruction because the Duke sent help to put the fires out and to tow the ship, the *San Salvador*, to safety inside the crescent. The other injured ship, the *Rosario*, was less fortunate. Rising squalls damaged her further and the Armada had to sail on into the darkness, leaving her to her fate.

When the short summer night ended, Drake saw, in the path of the rising sun, a great Spanish galleon, drifting helplessly with her foremast and bowsprit damaged. Her captain, Pedro de Valdés, finding that the English ship into whose guns they were looking was commanded by the famous Sir Francis Drake himself, surrendered the *Rosario* with courteous remarks about Drake's fame and generosity. She turned out to be one of the richest prizes and helped pay for the expenses of the English fleet.

James Campion of the *Isabel* was sure he could have taken the prize himself if he had only come up with her at the right moment. He told Oliver so as the *Isabel* and the *Rejoice* lay for a few moments becalmed, close beside each other.

"Why, you could have captured her yourself," James called across the water.

Most of the other English captains thought the same. Oliver, however, was doubtful about it.

"That's because at heart you are just a farmer," James called.

James was in great spirits. The Armada, so far as James was concerned, had sailed for England chiefly for his entertainment. To dash in and out of the Spanish crescent and to bring Drake reports of what he had seen was the highest pleasure he could imagine. He would have attacked the *San Martin* single-handed if Drake had told him to.

Perhaps he was right in saying Oliver was a farmer at heart. By Monday afternoon, with the wind failing and neither fleet making headway, Oliver felt as if the battle had gone on forever, that it would always go on with nothing accomplished, that Parma's army would meet the Armada and nothing would stop them from invading England.

On Tuesday, however, things went, if not better, at least more swiftly. There was wind from the east. The Spaniards had the weather gauge. They almost succeeded in grappling English ships. Cannon on both sides smoked and roared. Through the smoke Oliver, carrying messages for Drake, caught glimpses of different parts of the day's fighting. Once he saw Frobisher in the *Triumph* attacked by several galleasses, but standing off until Lord Howard came to his aid.

He saw the *Ark Royal* and the *San Martin* come so close that Medina Sidonia had the *San Martin*'s topsails struck. This was the Duke's challenge to Lord Howard to fight it out single-handed. Instead of grappling, Howard formed his ships in line and sailed past the *San Martín*, each ship delivering a broadside as it passed. So much powder and shot was spent that day that Lord Howard and Drake sent messages ashore saying that they could fight no longer without fresh supplies. The Spaniards had not managed to grapple the English ships, but neither had the English cannon balls sunk the Spaniards. Both fleets patched up their damage. The Armada sailed on, still Invincible.

On Wednesday Oliver saw the *Gran Grifon*, one of the Spanish urcas, attacked by Drake. She was badly injured and many of her crew were killed and wounded but the galleasses rescued her and towed her back to the center of the crescent. The wind was so light that day that the two fleets drifted along eastward, hardly a mile apart. Pinnaces, the *Isabel* and the *Rejoice* among them, went back and forth between the English fleet and the shore, bringing cannon balls, cabbages and excited volunteers.

Oliver, carrying a message to Lord Howard, was on the *Ark Royal* while Howard was holding council. It was decided to divide the fleet into four squadrons. The commanders chosen were the Lord Admiral, Drake, Hawkins and Frobisher.

On Thursday there were new engagements. Once more Frobisher in the *Triumph* managed to slip away from Spaniards who almost grappled him. Drake and Hawkins attacked the outer edge of the crescent and drove the Spaniards so close inshore that they came near being wrecked on a dangerous bank—the Ower Bank—near the Isle of Wight. Drake feared that Medina Sidonia might seize the Isle of Wight and invade England from there, but the great crescent passed it, moving slowly eastward with the English at their heels.

The Lord Admiral felt that Thursday's fight against the

Armada was a victory. He called his captains to the deck of the *Ark Royal*. Drake with Oliver and James behind him saw Hawkins and Frobisher knighted. They had, Lord Howard said, taken part in the greatest battle ever fought at sea. Never had fleets of so many sails met before. Never had so many guns been fired.

This was true. Yet the Armada, in spite of the English cannon, was still the strongest fleet that had ever sailed the seas when, on Saturday afternoon, its ships suddenly struck sails and dropped anchor in Calais Roads.

CHAPTER 17

SHIPS OF FLAME

Medina Sidonia must have hoped, when the Armada dropped anchor so suddenly, that the English fleet would be carried past him by tide, wind and surprise. He must have been disappointed when English anchors dropped almost as fast as his own and the two fleets faced each other little more than a cannon shot apart.

They still faced each other on Sunday morning, July 28, when Lord Howard hung out his flag for a council. The English fleet was larger than before. A squadron that had been sailing the Channel to keep Parma from joining the Duke now added thirty-five more ships to the main fleet. Five of them were Queen's galleons. The English fleet was now almost as large as the Armada.

The council decided promptly to use fire ships against the Spaniards. The first plan was to send to Dover for ships and materials. As usual, Sir Francis Drake—that impatient, hasty man—wanted immediate action. A south south-east wind was rising. There would be a spring tide. The messenger was already on his way to Dover when Drake offered one of his own ships, the *Thomas*, two hundred tons. His cousin, Sir John Hawkins, was equally generous. So were six other commanders. One of them was Oliver Barrett, captain of the *Rejoice*.

It was, after all, Drake's ship, but Drake knew how hard it was to lose a first command and he had not asked for it. He had not needed to ask. All he did was to look at the *Rejoice* with his bright blue eyes and say, "Fire ships need not be big, so long as they are good brisk sailers."

The *Rejoice*, like the other fire ships, was soon being emptied of water and biscuit casks and filled instead with tar, tarred rope, oakum, tallowy rags, shavings, straw and gunpowder. They left her spars, rigging and sails. Her own guns were double-shotted and would go off when the flames reached them. Other loaded guns too were placed on her deck. By night she was ready.

There was a moon that night but ragged black clouds were blowing across it. When it shone clear for a moment, Oliver could see a line of Spanish pinnaces sailing between the two fleets. The Duke evidently expected fire ships. His pinnaces would try to grapple the burning ships and tow them into shallow water as Drake's pinnaces had done at Cadiz.

It was not until after midnight that the eight fire ships sailed. The spring tide was running swiftly by then and the wind rose with it, filling the sails of the line of lighted ships. As they sped on towards the anchored Armada, flames began to run up their ropes. Oliver, watching from the deck of the *Isabel*, saw the *Rejoice*'s sails like pink clouds in a smoky haze that almost hid the sails of the Armada. The eight ships sailed so close together that they seemed steered by ghostly helmsmen who could have tossed blazing balls of pitch and tow from one ship to the next. Beyond them Oliver could see the Spanish pinnaces waiting, shadowy in the glare.

"Look," James said, "they dare not come close to the ships in the center. They'd be scorched from two ships at once. They'll try to haul off the first one in the line and the last... Ah! That's seamanship!"

It was indeed a feat of seamanship for the Spanish pinnaces with wind, tide and the channel current all against them to grapple the two flaming ships and haul them towards the shore. One of them was a ship of more than a hundred tons. The other was the *Rejoice*. Oliver had left a pennant flying at her masthead. The fire had not yet reached it when, as the smoke blew aside, he caught one last glimpse of his ship close inshore.

He thought: So it was all for nothing!

Just then came the explosion. The *Rejoice*'s guns, heated by her burning deck, began to go off. Powder kegs exploded in her hold. Curtains of sparks blew towards the anchored Armada. Cannon balls struck close to the Spanish pinnaces. They were ready to seize another pair of fire ships, but the sound of cannon and the splashing shot, coming from all the flaming ships now, made them hesitate. The moment was lost. Six blazing, thundering ships swept down on the Armada. Through the smoke the exploding guns sent volcanoes of fire roaring towards the sky.

The Spanish galleons had their sails set. A gun from the *San Martín* signaled the Armada to leave its anchorage for the open channel but this time the great crescent did not form around him. Dreading flames and shot, the Spanish captains cut their cables and sailed as wind and tide took them, anywhere to be out of reach of the exploding fire ships.

For the first time the Spanish fleet was no longer like an army marching by sea instead of by land. Now it was only a disorderly lot of ships being swept towards the sands of the Low Countries by the strong current and the wind.

When dawn came the only Spanish ships still facing the English were the *San Martín*, four royal galleons of Portugal, and a galleass, the *San Lorenzo*, her rudder useless from a collision in the panic caused by the fire ships, close inshore.

Trumpets sounded on both fleets, sails were set, flags and pennants snapped in the wind. In the night the *San Lorenzo* had lost her anchor and been driven aground. Lord Howard and his squadron surrounded her, leaving Drake and the other commanders to pursue the rest of the Armada.

For the first time that Monday, July 29th, the fighting was in rough weather. They called it afterwards the Battle of Gravelines, a place north of Calais on the French coast. When the *Revenge* sailed past the *San Martín* and poured a broadside into her, the Duke answered with all his guns. Drake's other ships followed, all at close range, all firing their guns. The *San Martín* was hit often, yet she still fought on. Farther east other galleons, which had scattered when the fire ships came, were struggling to keep off the lee shore and to rejoin the Duke's squadron. Drake made it hard for them to do so, but some succeeded and the Spanish fleet was strengthened.

Frobisher in the *Triumph* had his turn at attacking the *San Martín*. Then Hawkins came in the *Victory* but the Spanish flagship still defied them like a wounded lion beating off a pack of dogs. Soon Hawkins found that the *San Martín* was forming a half-moon of ships round her.

"There may be fifteen," James Campion, who was scouting for Drake in the *Isabel*, said to Oliver. He added, "I think your

Duke is no longer seasick. I doubt if he has a cold in his head. He's a seaman!"

"High praise and he deserves it," Oliver said, "though he's not my Duke."

"He is your Duke, Mr Inky Fingers! Why, the very wind that blows across Cadiz is called the Medina because it comes from his country. Certainly he's your Duke and mine too and I'm proud of him. He hasn't enough ships to make his great crescent with as many masts as a porcupine's bristles, but he's made a small half-moon and I dare not go between its tips, I vow. When we beat him, we can be proud."

"Shall we beat him?" Oliver asked.

"Yes," James said. "We are no braver but our ships are more weatherly. Our guns are better and we still have cannon balls. Theirs are running low. Look!"

A great Spanish ship drove past them tossed by wind and waves so that the blood ran out of her scuppers and stained the foam around her. None of her big guns spoke but the men in her towers still fired their muskets at an English ship that pursued her. Still bleeding she staggered into place in the half-moon.

Just then came a violent burst of wind and driving fountains of rain. The English had enough to do to keep from smashing into each other. When the rain stopped and they could see the half-moon again, it was still moving northwards defiantly and doggedly.

"I said the Duke was a seaman!" said James Campion. "See— he's shortening sail. He's challenging us to attack again."

The English did not accept the challenge. It was now late afternoon and they had been fighting since dawn. They too were running short of ammunition. The *Isabel* carried a message from Drake to Walsingham.

It said, "God hath given us so good a day in forcing the enemy so far to leeward as I hope the Prince of Parma and the Duke of Medina Sidonia shall not shake hands this few days and whensoever they meet, I believe neither of them shall greatly rejoice in this day's service."

The letter ended with a plea for food and ammunition. Without more cannon balls they could not hope to sink the Armada. The best they could do was to follow it, edging it always to leeward, hoping to drive it on the Zeeland sands.

Early on Tuesday the *Isabel* was in sight of Boston Stump. James asked Drake's permission to land and try to get food and ammunition and to fill his water casks. The *Isabel* was soon lying at Oliver's own wharf near Campions'. James was rowed across to Boston to try to buy cannon balls. Stephen Barrett had his workmen load boats with everything the manor had on hand—carrots, cabbages, cheese, fruit, fowls, smoked hams—while Oliver and the crew filled the water casks and got supplies of firewood.

James was less successful. There was little powder and shot in Boston and the Mayor wished to keep what he had to fire at the Spaniards. However, he grudgingly parted with some of his supply on James's promise that it would be given to Drake himself.

He certainly did not trust little James Campion to do much against the Armada. James was a foot taller than the Mayor but to him James was still a mischievous choirboy. Drake was another matter.

Mistress Barrett felt differently. To her the *Isabel* was the most important ship in the English fleet. She was convinced it would chase the Armada away. She was worried only about Oliver and James catching cold. There was going to be a change in the weather, she said. She could feel it in her elbows. She gave them a flask containing her special mixture of herbs, honey and Spanish wine, excellent for coughs. They must just add hot water to it.

Oliver remembered it well. He would have liked to go to bed at Campions' with a poultice on his chest, a hot brick at his feet and plenty of cough mixture, but he went back to chasing the Armada almost before he came, as his mother complained, and they ate almost nothing. She over looked all the bread and ale the crew consumed and the bread and cream and strawberry jam Oliver and James ate walking through the garden. There was still a bridle of roses on the Knight's green horse and the elephant still raised his trunk.

"Where is Joyce?" James asked.

The answer was what Oliver feared it would be.

Joyce, Mistress Barrett said, had gone to Tweedmouth again. One of her cousin's ships had stopped at Boston two weeks ago and Joyce had sailed in it to make another visit. No, there was nothing new about the marriage. The leather merchant still demanded a dowry. It was a fine chance for Joyce. As soon as James and Oliver had beaten the Spaniards, the leather business would be good again. James really ought to help his sister.

"Does she like this leather merchant?" James asked. "How old is he?"

"A suitable age for the head of a family," Mistress Barrett said. "His first wife had six children. He is about forty-seven—but my cousin writes me that he appears much younger," she added hastily. "Now if you will just capture one of those Spanish galleons—there must be plenty at hand—you could give her a good dowry. And Oliver, you promised to do something for her."

"True," James said. "Doubtless he will if we catch a Spanish ship. We had better start or we'll lose track of them."

He called his men and they were soon at sea again under full sail with Boston Stump melting away in the clouds behind them. Before long the *Isabel* had come up with the *Revenge* and James had handed over the Mayor's cannon balls.

The Armada was now close to the lee shore, with the English fleet under shortened sail slowly and relentlessly driving it towards the Zeeland sands. The Spanish leadsmen were sounding the shallow water. The *San Martín* must, Oliver thought, draw at least five fathoms of water. He could hear a leadsman calling seven fathoms when the wind suddenly shifted. It blew the Armada off the sands where the waves would have smashed it more quickly than cannon balls. In a few moments the whole fleet was safe in deep water and still moving northward.

So the victory was not yet won. Council was held on the *Ark Royal* that night. We must still pursue the Spaniards, Lord Howard said, until we are sure they will not seize an English or a Scottish port. Drake and the other captains agreed that their business was to keep the Armada from the shores of England. So both fleets sailed northward, past Hull, past Tweedmouth, past Berwick.

At last on August 2nd the Lord Admiral decided that the Spaniards would not try to land. Except for a few scouting ships—the *Isabel* was one of them—the English headed for the Firth of Forth to rest and refit before turning south.

The Armada sailed on.

ESTRELLITA

Now there were no galleons left to be captured even by Drake, even by James Campion. Those last cannon balls would never splinter Spanish oak. During that night even the *Isabel* lost track of the Armada and, after sailing north on Tuesday without seeing a Spanish sail, at last turned south to keep the rendezvous Drake had given them on the Thames near Tilbury.

There were still signs in the North Sea that the greatest fleet that ever sailed had passed that way. Once, not far from the Firth of Forth, they saw a ship's boat, one that Oliver might have rowed in Cadiz, floating upside down on the gray water. A little further south was a tangled wreckage of sails and spars being carried inland by the waves and, as they watched, the figurehead of a Spanish ship rose like a cold mermaid beside them, then plunged back and was dashed away towards the shore.

The wind had veered round now. As they sailed into the North Sea they saw something stranger than any mermaid. All round them the sea was full of swimming horses struggling in the waves. The cavalry that was to carry fire and sword through England would never ride now. Those proud horses, like the one Don Alfonso rode in Cadiz, which would have carried the cavaliers, were drowning. All that night the wind shrieked and Oliver, at the *Isabel's* helm or half asleep in his bunk, kept dreading and dreaming that he heard the gasp of dying horses.

The sea was empty of them when dawn came, a chilly watery dawn but with less wind. The waves were no longer gray mountains topped with snow. By noon pale sunshine sparkled on green water. There were no other ships in sight. They could see land now, an island with a few trees twisted by the wind and a sandy cove between steep rocky headlands edged with green turf.

Oliver saw sheep nibbling the turf—and something else.

He heard James say, "There's a strong current setting in towards the island. We must come about."

"No!" Oliver said. "You must land me. Drop anchor."

He spoke in a tone so strange that for a moment James stared at him without giving the order either to come about or anchor. The *Isabel* was now in the lee of the northern headland in quiet water. No wind filled her sails, but she moved slowly with the current towards the white beach. There was nothing to do but anchor and James gave the order. As the anchors splashed into the water he said to Oliver, "Are you mad?"

"No, Master Campion, I am not mad. I ask for the hand of your sister in marriage."

"What?"

"And I am going ashore to get her wedding present."

James stared at him and at last stammered, "What—what's that about Joyce?"

"You did not really think I'd let her marry that leather merchant, did you?"

"No," James said.

"Wouldn't you rather she married me? In case she loves me, of course."

"Yes."

"Well, what are we waiting for? Let's go ashore and fetch her golden horse. Look!"

James spun around and looked where Oliver pointed.

Just where the turf met the white sand the golden horse was grazing. Her coat was still rough and salty and darkened from the sea, but where the sun had dried it pale, gold was beginning to show and her mane and tail were silver. One of her delicate forefeet was white and she had a white star on her forehead.

She raised her head as the ship's boat touched the shore and stared at it with gentle almost mournful eyes. They looked very large. She pawed the grass lightly with her white foot and shook her silvery mane. Around her arched neck, the reins looped and knotted, was a bridle of Spanish leather shining with gold and silver.

"Hurry," James said as Oliver started slowly across the beach, "or she'll run away!"

Oliver did not hurry. He had a bunch of carrots from the garden at Campions' in his hand. He took a bite of one and held out the rest of it towards the mare. She sniffed and tossed her head as if to say, "Carrots? Really, I'm not sure if I care for a carrot just now. Of course, I know they're good for the coat—"

Oliver edged forwards a little. He bit off another piece of carrot. It was so quiet on the island that James could hear him crunch it between his teeth. The horse twitched her ears and stepped towards him. Every motion she made was graceful. In

a moment her thin soft lips lightly touched Oliver's palm as she took the carrot. She ate it as elegantly as Queen Elizabeth would eat a marchpane with her gold and crystal fork, he thought.

Oliver stroked her salty, roughened mane. She hardly seemed to notice when he laid his hand on the bridle and she politely accepted another carrot which she ate while he stood beside her talking to her in Spanish and English.

"Estrellita d'oro—little golden star—palomina mia—my little dove," he said.

"What are you going to do with your little dove now?" James asked.

After all, to James a horse was only a horse. No matter if this one was a great-great-granddaughter of one of Queen Isabella's golden horses. No matter if—as Oliver told him—her ancestors were royal Arabs before the Plantagenets were Kings of England. How did Oliver know she was an Arab? Oh, she had only five ribs instead of six? And how did he know that? Oh, Don Alfonso de Rodríguez, Old Bazán's secretary? And would Don Alfonso help get her on board the *Isabel*? She was after all only a horse and horses were bad enough on land where they belonged but at sea—!

"She'll probably be seasick," James said gloomily.

"Seasick! A horse that swam to shore in that storm!"

"The current helped her," James said.

"Estrellita d'oro," said Oliver, "is a sea horse."

The *Isabel's* boat was a sturdy one. Estrellita d'oro, as Oliver pointed out, weighed no more than a load of cannon balls. She stepped into the boat as neatly as if she rode in one every day. She did not mind being slung on board the *Isabel*. She nuzzled Oliver's hand gently as the tackle was being rigged. She seemed to enjoy the ship.

"She acts as if she owns it," James said. "Where will Her Majesty condescend to sail now?"

"Why, to Tweedmouth," said Oliver. "To see her new mistress and to take her home."

Joyce seemed to have no objection to leaving Tweedmouth. Like Estrellita she enjoyed the *Isabel*. It would be hard to say who was happiest as they sailed south for Boston—Oliver or Joyce or Estrellita d'oro. James, of course, muttered, "Horses! Horses!" from time to time and complained that the wisps of hay and scattering of oats brought from Tweedmouth made his ship look like a stable. However, even he admitted that, for a horse, Estrellita was not bad to have aboard; better than a goat or an elephant or an ostrich, he said. Joyce cheerfully accepted these remarks as compliments and went on grooming Estrellita's coat. She soon had it looking like gold satin. She brushed the horse's tail and mane till each strand of hair was like silvery silk. Estrellita stayed happily in the box Oliver had built for her to keep her safe from storms, but every day Joyce led her out of the box, bridled her and mounted her and sat looking out to sea. When they reached the wharf at Campions' Joyce rode Estrellita off the ship, speaking to her so that the horse seemed to understand that she was at home.

Oliver walked along beside them. When they came out through the clipped yews to the open sunny terrace, he said, "I always thought this terrace needed something."

"Oh," Joyce cried. "What is it, Oliver? I must get it for you!"

"The statue of a golden horse with you on its back, but I like the real one better."

Mistress Barrett was delighted to see Joyce. She fell in love at once with Estrellita, though she was disappointed that James had not captured a galleon.

"I suppose there's no chance of Master Higginbotham now," she said while Joyce and Oliver were taking Estrellita to the stable.

Master Higginbotham was the leather merchant.

"No," James said. "There's no hope."

"Oliver always said he'd do something for her," Mistress Barrett said.

"He's going to," said James. "He's going to make her mistress of Campions'. They'll be married as soon as Drake lets him go. I have given my consent."

Something strange happened. Mistress Barrett was struck silent. However, she recovered rapidly.

"I knew it," she said. "I knew it all the time."

Stephen Barrett, however, was astonished and admitted it. Joyce was delighted when he told her and Oliver that he had not been so amazed since Frankie came back from seizing the mule trains of Panama with his pockets full of quoits of gold.

"Where is Frankie—that is, Sir Francis now?" he asked.

"He gave us a rendezvous at the mouth of the Thames near Tilbury," Oliver said. "We must keep it soon. Parma may still cross the Channel or the Armada might sail south again. I think we have seen the last of them, but we must still be on our guard and we must make our report to Drake."

Mistress Barrett was rather disappointed to think that the Armada had vanished. She liked to feel that there was still a chance that they might pick up a Spanish galleon—not that they needed it so much now that Master Higginbotham, that stingy, wizened little leather merchant, did not have to be purchased.

Master Higginbotham was actually a tall, comfortable looking man, Joyce said, but Mistress Barrett had lost interest in him.

"I never thought him good enough for you. I don't know what your cousins were thinking of," she said, and added that Joyce must stay at home now and not go running off visiting on every ship that came into Boston Harbor. The manor was going to pieces without her. Why, the last time she set out a pan of milk not enough cream rose on it to feed a butterfly.

She was still giving sad reports about the manor—though Oliver thought he had never seen it looking better—when the *Isabel* left Campions' Wharf and slipped off into Boston Deeps with the tide.

Joyce had ridden Estrellita down to the wharf. The last

thing Oliver saw as the *Isabel* rounded the next point was the sun shining on Joyce's red-gold hair and on Estrellita's pale gold coat.

"Next time I come home it will be to stay," he said to James, who replied that there was no accounting for tastes.

When they reached the rendezvous they found Drake on the deck of the *Revenge* and made their report. They had kept the Armada in sight till they were sure it would not turn back. They told him about the swimming horses.

One of the urcas, a troop-ship carrying cavalry horses, might have sunk, Oliver thought.

Drake said, "I think horses on more than one ship may have been thirsty and men pushed them overboard to save what water they could for themselves. Come! See who is in my cabin."

A small man sat writing at the cabin table. Even before he turned Oliver knew that bent back, the head with the reddish-brown hair, showing gray now.

He said, "Juan Enríquez—Master!" and found himself looking into the printer's bright kind eyes.

He had come across from Dunkirk only that morning, John Hendricks said. He was writing his report for Secretary Walsingham. He was telling him that the Armada was short of ammunition, food and water. They had bought some food while they were anchored near Calais and had filled a few water casks, but the governor had refused to sell them powder and shot, and the fire ships had scattered the fleet before it was well provisioned.

"It was burning those good barrel staves near Cape St Vincent that damaged the Armada most," Hendricks said. "The green ones they had to use shrank. Casks leaked. Mice and weevils got into the biscuit. Meat spoiled. It hurt the Duke more than sinking a dozen galleons.

"A man who got ashore from a ship wrecked on the sands of Zeeland told me about it.

"'The Duke is a brave man,' he said, 'and a good commander, but he's seen enough of the English fleet. He'll never come back with half-starved crews and no shot to meet it.'

"The Armada is more damaged than Lord Howard thinks," Hendricks went on. "The Duke will make his way around Scotland and Ireland and get as many ships as he can back to Spain. A man from the galleass *San Lorenzo* told me so. He spoke about the leaking casks and he said that after the fire ships scattered the Armada there was no hope for it."

Oliver thought of the *Rejoice* speeding towards the Armada with flames running up her ropes.

My first command—and my last one, he thought.

John Hendricks was saying that Parma would never come out now.

"The Dutch have him bottled up. Even if he wished to come—and I doubt if he does—he could not. Englishmen can begin to sleep quietly at night. It is a great victory."

Drake believed him. Others did not. The army at Tilbury still stayed to meet Parma if he set foot on English soil. In August the Queen set out from London to inspect the army at Tilbury. Londoners crowded London Bridge and the banks of the Thames to see the royal barge go by. As the silver trumpets sounded, the shouts of the crowd began and followed her all the way. She was escorted by the yeomen of the guard and by the gentlemen of her household in shining armor.

Members of her council decided that she might inspect the army but from a safe distance and well guarded.

Elizabeth decided otherwise. When she inspected the troops the Earl of Ormonde went first, carrying her sword. Two pages in white velvet came next. One carried her silver helmet, the other led her horse.

Oliver and James, watching in a group of other ship captains, heard the shouts as she came in sight and began to cheer more loudly than anyone. There were no armed guards around her, only the Earl of Leicester riding on one side, the Earl of Essex on the other and Sir John Norris behind. She rode a white horse and she was dressed in white velvet with a breastplate of silver.

She had changed very little since Oliver had seen her first at Kenilworth, and the words of her speech made him think of her voice when he first knew she was the Queen.

This was her speech:

"My loving people. We have been persuaded by some that are careful for our safety to take heed how we commit ourselves to armed multitudes for fear of treachery. But I assure you, I do not desire to live to distrust my faithful and loving people. Let tyrants fear! I have always so behaved myself that, under God, I have placed my chiefest strength and safeguard in the loyal hearts and goodwill of my subjects, and therefore I am come amongst you, as you see, resolved in the midst and heat of battle to live or die amongst you all, and to lay down, for my God, for my kingdom and for my people, my honor and my blood even in the dust. I know I have the body of a weak and feeble woman but I have the heart of a King, and a King of England too, and think foul scorn that Parma or Spain, or any prince of Europe should dare invade the borders of my realm. To which rather than that any dishonor shall grow by me, I myself will take up arms, I myself will be your general, judge and rewarder of everyone of your virtues in the field. I know already you have deserved rewards and crowns; and we do assure you, on the word of a prince, they shall be duly paid you."

The shouts from her people were so loud that if the whole Invincible Armada had shot off its guns no one would have heard.

As she rode away she saw Drake in the crowd and called him to her. James had gone back to the *Isabel*, but Oliver was still with his master.

"Come with me," Drake said to him.

The crowd shouted, "Drake! Drake! Hey, Frankie—you sent them running! God bless you, Sir Francis!" and good naturedly stood aside making a path for them.

The Queen said, "Sir Francis Drake, we have much for which to thank you, for chasing the Armada from our shores, especially for your fire ships which, we understand, did much distress and scatter the enemy."

Drake thanked her for what she said and added, "And here is Oliver Barrett, captain of one of the fire ships, his first command gladly given in Your Majesty's service."

The Queen turned her piercing blue gaze on Oliver.

"Why," she said, "and he brought my lute—which was 'more of a cittern really'!—and circled the globe in our service. Come, Drake, he deserves something from us. Give us our sword!" she said to the Earl of Ormonde.

When she received it, she handed it to Drake saying, "Come! We must make a knight of him."

Oliver, his head spinning, knelt in the dust. He felt Drake tap him on the shoulder, thought James, it should have been James—not me, and heard the Queen's voice ring out.

"Rise, Sir Oliver Barrett," it said and he got to his feet, hearing the crowd cheering, not so much for him, he knew, as for Drake and the Queen.

So when the corn was cut at Campions' and standing in golden sheaves, Joyce Campion became Lady Barrett. They were married in Boston Stump and James was there to give his sister away and to be Oliver's groomsman too. James had a new ship to command now, a galleon of Drake's.

When Oliver said to him, "You should be the knight, James," James only laughed and said cheerfully, "Oh, knights are better ashore with hayseed in their beards and carrying buttermilk to the pigs. I'd rather have my galleon than all the pigs in Lincolnshire."

He had called his new ship the *Isabel* after the old one. It was a lucky name, he said.

"I wonder what happened to the real Isabel," he said as he and Oliver stood in the cabin of the galleon. "Did you ever hear?"

Oliver told him that he heard she had married a cousin of the Marquis of Santa Cruz and lived in Seville, but he did not tell him how she looked.

"Do you remember her dancing?" James said.

"Yes," said Oliver.

He would never tell James that Isabel had turned into a fat, disagreeable Spanish lady. It was better, he thought, for James to remember her on her black horse at Campions' or at Kenilworth dancing the pavane in the light of a thousand candles.

Among the wedding guests who had sailed to Boston with James were Sir Francis Drake and John Hendricks. Drake had come only partly for the wedding, he said. He wished to give the Queen something beautiful at the New Year and he had thought of something. One of Stephen Barrett's workmen must make it. The plumes, he said, came from Patagonia. It must be different from any other ever made, he said. He was so eloquent about it that the bells of Boston Stump began to ring for the wedding while he was still talking.

However, there was still time for Mistress Barrett to scold Drake and her husband, for Joyce to ride to the church on Estrellita, for Oliver to ask James where the wedding ring was and for James to say soothingly, "Patience, Sir Oliver, it is on the little finger of my left hand. Come, let me not hear such knocking of knees and chattering of teeth. The Invincible Armada is back in Spain. What do you fear?"

So they were safely married and they rode back to the manor, Joyce on Estrellita, Oliver on a large bay horse sometimes used for plowing. They had the best dinner, Drake said, that he had eaten since his last visit, and music and dancing afterwards. James sang "Pastime with Good Company" and Oliver played the cittern. Estrellita put her head through an open casement and listened happily.

Stephen Barrett and Drake and John Hendricks talked together in words that carried them from the stranded hulks where they had lived as small boys to the ends of the earth and home again. They talked too about the Queen's New Year's gift.

In January, 1589, among the treasures she received was: "A fan of feathers white and red, the handle of gold, enameled with a half-moon of mother of pearl, within that a half-moon garnished with sparks of diamonds and a few seed pearls on one side, having Her Majesty's picture within it; and on the back a device with a crow over it. Given by Sir Francis Drake."

Joyce held it in her hand before it was sent to London. It was beautiful with the ostrich plumes combining the white rose of York and the red rose of Lancaster with the shining of gold and pearls and diamonds.

"We'll make you one like it," Stephen Barrett said. "Oliver still has plumes he brought from Patagonia."

"No," Joyce said. "There must be only one. She is the Queen and she has so little. I have so much."

LAST VOYAGE

JAMES SAILED with Drake on all his voyages. Twice in the next six years he sailed into Boston Harbor and visited Campions'. Once he found a small redheaded boy playing with a golden foal with a silvery mane and tail. The boy was almost five years old and his name was James Campion Barrett, he said, and the foal's name was Sir Francis. Yes, he said, he liked horses, but he liked the sea better. The tall man who had come off the big galleon lying in the harbor seemed much pleased with this remark. He told it to everyone he met. He even said it in Spanish to Estrellita.

He brought a Spanish book and gave it to John Hendricks, who lived at Campions'. After supper in the long summer evenings Oliver Barrett read aloud from this book. He would put his spectacles on his nose and he turned the Spanish words into English. Even in English young James did not understand them completely. The story was about a knight called Don Quixote and James liked to hear about him, though his father, the only knight he knew, was not much like him. He supposed Spaniards must be different.

James Barrett did not see his uncle again for a long time. He always remembered the day a letter came from him and his mother crying as his father read it aloud. The letter was about Sir Francis Drake, whom his grandfather sometimes called Frankie and then corrected himself. In the stories Stephen Barrett used to tell James about his friend—Fortune's Child, he sometimes called him—Drake was always victorious. He went through great hardships but he always came home with ships full of gold for the Queen. He sailed round the world—so did my father, James Barrett thought. He chased the Armada away from England— and so did my father. This story was different. Because my father was not there—James thought.

He heard the names of towns Drake had attacked. Puerto Rico, Santa Marta, Nombre de Dios. They found no treasure anywhere. They tried to capture Panama and failed. Rain soaked their powder. They were half starved. Many were ill with fever. Drake himself was ill when the expedition came back from Panama. The failure was terrible to him.

He wondered [James Campion wrote] that since coming out of England he never saw sail worth giving chase to. Yet, in the greatness of his mind he would say, "It matters not, man; God hath many things in store for us; and I know many means to do Her Majesty good service, for we must have gold before we see England."

Since our return from Panama he never carried mirth nor joy in his face; yet no man he loved must show that he took thought thereof. We came to Porta Bella, which is within nine leagues of Nombre de Dios. It was the best harbor we came into since Plymouth. Our Captain was very ill of a fever and the next morning at seven o'clock he died. The next day we buried him in the sea in a coffin sealed with lead and weighted with round shot. We sunk two ships beside him for him to command on his voyage.

Fortune's Child was dead. We knew things would not fall into our mouths nor riches be our portion, how dearly soever we adventured for them. So on March 8th the fleet shot the Gulf and came for England, leaving Florida astern, and when we came to the Enchanted Islands we were dispersed and came home one by one.

He was in Plymouth, he wrote. He would sail to Boston and see them all in a few weeks now.

The letter ended:

You asked me when last I saw you, Joyce, if we really conquered that Invincible Armada. Then I vowed we had; now I am less sure. Spain is strong at sea. Her towns in the Indies are guarded all too well. Her treasure from Peru comes safely to Spain.

It may be all the Armada did was to test our courage— and what is a man without courage? Years from now we may say in days of fear, "Our Queen had a brave heart as did Sir Francis Drake." What! Shall we forget all we learned from them? I pray not. And I am your loving friend and brother—who kisses your hands and pulls your son's hair and the silver mane of Estrellita d'oro and of her son.

Yours,

J. Campion

Oliver Barrett folded the letter. He saw through a mist the Armada marching on the sea in the great crescent, the lighted beacons smoking across England, the fire ships roaring in flames. He saw the table in the cabin of the *Golden Hind* set with dishes of silver and gold and Drake helping a Spanish don from his own plate.

"Keep this letter, James," he said to his son. "It is worth more than gold."